Also by David Malouf

Fiction
The Complete Stories
Every Move You Make
Dream Stuff
The Conversations at Curlow Creek
Remembering Babylon
The Great World
Antipodes
Harland's Half Acre
Child's Play
Fly Away Peter
An Imaginary Life
Johnno

Autobiography
12 Edmondstone Street

Poetry
Selected Poems
Wild Lemons
First Things Last
The Year of Foxes and Other Poems
Neighbours in a Thicket
Bicycle and Other Poems
Typewriter Music

Libretti
Jane Eyre
Baa Baa Black Sheep

RANSOM

RANSOM
DAVID
MALOUF

PANTHEON BOOKS · NEW YORK

Copyright © 2009 by David Malouf
All rights reserved. Published in the United States by
Pantheon Books, a division of Random House, Inc.,
New York. Originally published in Australia by
Random House Pty Ltd, Sydney, in 2009.

Pantheon Books and colophon are
registered trademarks of Random House, Inc.

Library of Congress Cataloging-in-Publication Data
Malouf, David, [date]
Ransom / David Malouf.
p.   cm.
ISBN 978-0-307-37877-4
1. Achilles (Greek mythology)—Fiction.
2. Priam (Greek mythology)—Fiction.
3. Loss (Psychology)—Fiction.
4. Greece—History—To 146 B.C.—Fiction.   I. Title.
PR9619.3.M265R36 2010   823'.914—dc22
2009020669

www.pantheonbooks.com

Printed in the United States of America
First United States Edition
2 4 6 8 9 7 5 3 1

RANSOM

The sea has many voices. The voice this man is listening for is the voice of his mother. He lifts his head, turns his face to the chill air that moves in across the gulf, and tastes its sharp salt on his lip. The sea surface bellies and glistens, a lustrous silver-blue – a membrane stretched to a fine transparency where once, for nine changes of the moon, he had hung curled in a dream of pre-existence and was rocked and comforted. He hunkers down now on the shelving pebbles at its edge, bunches his cloak between his thighs. Chin down, shoulders hunched, attentive.

The gulf can be wild at times, its voices so loud in a man's head that it is like standing stilled in the midst of battle. But today in the dawn light it is pondlike. Small waves slither to his sandalled feet, then sluice away with a rattling sound as the smooth stones loosen and go rolling.

The man is a fighter, but when he is not fighting he is a farmer, earth is his element. One day, he knows, he will go back to it. All the grains that were miraculously called together at his birth to make just these hands, these feet, this corded forearm, will separate and go their own ways again. He is a child of earth. But for the whole of his life he has been drawn, in his other nature, to his mother's element. To what, in all its many forms, as ocean, pool, stream, is shifting and insubstantial. To what accepts, in a moment of stillness, the reflection of a face, a tree in leaf, but holds nothing, and itself cannot be held.

As a child he had his own names for the sea. He would repeat them over and over under his breath as a way of calling to her till the syllables shone and became her presence. In the brimming moonlight of his sleeping chamber, at midday in his father's garden, among oakwoods when summer gales bullied and the full swing of afternoon came crashing, he felt himself caught up and tenderly enfolded as her low voice whispered on his skin. Do you hear me, Achilles? It is me, I am still with you. For a time I can be with you when you call.

He was five then, six. She was his secret. He floated in the long soft swirlings of her hair.

But she had warned him from the beginning that she would not always be with him. She had given him up. That was the hard condition of his being and of all commerce between them. One day when he put his foot down on the earth he knew at once that something was different. A gift he had taken as natural to him, the play of a dual self that had allowed him, in a moment, to slip out of his hard boyish nature and become eel-like, fluid, weightless, without substance in his mother's arms, had been withdrawn. From now on she would be no more than a faint far-off echo to his senses, an underwater humming.

He had grieved. But silently, never permitting himself to betray to others what he felt.

Somewhere in the depths of sleep his spirit had

made a crossing and not come back, or it had been snatched up and transformed. When he bent and chose a stone for his slingshot it had a new weight in his hand, and the sling had a different tension. He was his father's son and mortal. He had entered the rough world of men, where a man's acts follow him wherever he goes in the form of story. A world of pain, loss, dependency, bursts of violence and elation; of fatality and fatal contradictions, breathless leaps into the unknown; at last of death – a hero's death out there in full sunlight under the gaze of gods and men, for which the hardened self, the hardened body, had daily to be exercised and prepared.

A breeze touches his brow. Far out where the gulf deepens, small waves kick up, gather, then collapse, and new ones replace them; and this, even as he watches, repeats itself, and will do endlessly whether he is here or not to observe it: that is what he sees. In the long vista of time he might already be gone. It is time, not space, he is staring into.

For nine years winter and summer they have

been cooped up here on the beach, all the vast horde of them, Greeks of every clan and kingdom, from Argos and Sparta and Boeotia, from Euboea, Crete, Ithaca, Cos and the other islands, or like himself and his men, his Myrmidons, from Phthia. Days, years, season after season; an endless interim of keeping your weapons in good trim and your keener self taut as a bowstring through long stretches of idleness, of restless, patient waiting, and shameful quarrels and unmanly bragging and talk.

Such a life is death to the warrior spirit. Which if it is to endure at the high point needs action – the clash of arms that settles a quarrel quickly, then sends a man back, refreshed in spirit, to being a good farmer again.

War should be practised swiftly, decisively. Thirty days at most, in the weeks between new spring growth and harvest, when the corn is tinder-dry and ripe for the invader's brand, then back to the cattle pace of the farmer's life. To calendar days and what comes with them; to seedtime and plough-ing and the garnering of grain. To tramping in your old sandals across sunstruck fields, all dry sticks and the smell of wild mint underfoot. To sitting about in the shade doling out the small change of gossip, and listening, while flies buzz and the sweat streams from your armpits, to interminable disputes – the administering of justice on home ground. To pruning olives, and watching, over months, the swelling of a broodmare's belly or the sprouting of the first pale blade among sods. To noting how far a son has grown since last year's notch on a doorjamb.

In these nine years his own son, Neoptolemus, away there in his grandfather's house, has been growing up without him. Days, weeks, season after season.

The sun is climbing now. He pushes to his feet. Stands for a last moment filled with his thoughts; his mind, even in its passive state, the most active part of him. Then, head down, his cloak drawn close about him, starts back along the sloping beach towards the camp.

There is a singing in the air, so high-pitched that it might be spirits. It comes from the rigging of the ships that swing at anchor, recent arrivals, or are drawn up in pinewood cradles along the strand.

There are more than a thousand of them. Their spars, in silhouette against the pallid sky, are like a forest magically transported. After so many months ashore, their hulls are white as bone. They stretch in a line back to the camp, and on the sea side make one of its walls.

He moves quickly now, it is cold out of the sun. Walking awkwardly against the slope of the beach, he has a drunken gait. His sandals slip on the pebbles, some of which are as large and smooth as duck eggs. Between them, brown-gold bladderwrack still damp from the tide.

When the last of the line of ships is behind him, he pauses and takes a long look out across the gulf. The sea, all fire, spreads flat to the horizon. So solid-looking and without depth, so enticing as a place to move to, that a man might be tempted to make a sharp turn right and try walking on it, and only when it opened and took him down discover he had been tricked by a freak of nature.

But the sea is not where it will end. It will end here on the beach in the treacherous shingle, or out there on the plain. That is fixed, inevitable. With the pious resignation of the old man he will never become, he has accepted this.

But in some other part of himself, the young man he is resists, and it is the buried rage of that resistance that drives him out each morning to tramp the shore. Not quite alone. With his ghosts.

Patroclus, his soulmate and companion since childhood.

Hector, implacable enemy.

Patroclus had simply appeared one afternoon in his father's court, a boy three years older than himself and nearly a head taller. Thin-jawed, intense, with the hands and feet, already disproportionately large, of the man he was growing into.

Achilles had been hunting in one of the ravines beyond the palace. He had killed a hare. Great whoops of triumph preceding him, he had come bounding up the steps into the courtyard to show his father what he had got.

Ten years old. Long-haired, wiry, burnt black by the Phthian sun. Still half-wild. His soul not yet settled in him.

Peleus was angry at the intrusion. He turned to

reprove the boy, but gentled when he saw what it was. He gestured to Achilles to be still. Then, with a small helpless showing of his palms – You see what it is, I too am a fond parent – apologised to his guest, Menoetius, King of Opus, for this unintended discourtesy.

Achilles, still panting from his long run in across the fields, set himself to be patient. Idly at first, with no intimation of what all this would one day mean to him, assuming still that the centre of the occasion was the hare trailing gouts of blood where it hung from his wrist, he stood shifting from foot to foot, waiting for the visitor's business to be done and his father's attention to be his.

The story Menoetius had to tell was a shocking one.

The boy with the big hands and feet was his son, Patroclus. Ten days ago, in a quarrel over a game of knucklebones, he had struck and killed one of his companions, the ten-year-old son of Amphidamas, a high official of the royal court. Menoetius was bringing the boy to Phthia as an outcast seeking asylum.

In a voice still hollow with wonder at how, in an instant, so many lives could be flung about and broken, the unhappy man led them back to the fatal morning.

Two players, fiercely engaged in the rivalries of the game, squatting in the shade of a colonnade and laughing. Taunting one another as young boys will. Eyes raised to follow the knucklebones as they climb, with nothing untoward in view.

For a long moment the taws hang there at the top of their flight; as if, in the father's grave retelling of these events, he were allowing for a gap to be opened where this time round some higher agency might step in and, with the high-handed indifference of those who have infinite power over the world of conjunction and accident, reverse what is about to occur. The silence is screwed up a notch. Even the cicadas have shut off mid-shriek.

The boy whose fate is suspended here stands with parted lips, though no breath passes between them; lost, as they all are, in a story he might be hearing for the first time and which has not yet found its end.

Achilles, too, stands spellbound. Like a sleeper who has stumbled in on another's dream, he sees what is about to happen but can neither move nor cry out to prevent it. His right arm is so heavy (he has forgotten the hare) that he may never lift it again. The blow is about to come.

The boy Patroclus tilts his chin, thin brows drawn in expectation, a little moisture lighting the down on his upper lip, and for the first time Achilles meets his gaze. Patroclus looks at him. The blow connects, bone on bone. And the boy, his clear eyes still fixed on Achilles, takes it. With just a slight jerk of the shoulders, an almost imperceptible intake of breath.

Achilles is as stunned as if the blow was to himself. He turns quickly to his father, on whose word so much depends.

But there is no need to add his own small weight of entreaty. Peleus too is moved by the spectacle of this boy with the mark of the outcast upon him, the brand of the killer, who stands waiting in a kind of no-man's-land to be readmitted to the companionship of men.

So it was settled. Patroclus was to be his adoptive brother, and the world, for Achilles, reassembled itself around a new centre. His true spirit leapt forth and declared itself. It was as if he had all along needed this other before he could become fully himself. From this moment on he could conceive of nothing in the life he must live that Patroclus would not share in and approve.

But things did not always go smoothly between them. There were times when Patroclus was difficult to approach, too touchily aware that, for all Achilles' brotherly affection, he himself was a courtier, a dependant here. He would draw back, all pride and a hurt that could not easily be assuaged. What Achilles saw then on the clouded brow was what he had been so struck by in the first glance that had passed between them – the daunted look that had captured his soul before he even knew that he had one – and he would hear again, as if the memory were his own, what Patroclus was hearing: the knock of bone on bone as two lives collided and were irrevocably changed.

No, Achilles told himself, not two lives, three. Because when Patroclus relived the moment now, he too was there. Breath held, too dazed, too spiritbound to move, he looked on dreamlike as that other – the small son of Amphidamas, whose face he had never seen – was casually struck aside to make way for him.

He thought often of that boy. They were mated. But darkly, flesh to ghost. As in a different way, but through the same agency and in the same moment, he had been mated with Patroclus.

The end when it came was abrupt, though not entirely accidental.

After weeks of truce, the war had resumed with a new ferocity, at first in isolated skirmishes, then, when it emerged that there was division among the Greeks and that Achilles, the most formidable of them, had withdrawn his forces, in a general assault. Hector, slaughtering on all sides, had stormed the walls of the encampment and fought his way to the Greek ships. The Greek cause had become desperate.

So too had Patroclus. Held back from the fight because of Achilles' quarrel with the generals, he was going earnestly from place to place about the camp hearing news of the death of this man, the wounding to near death of another, all dear companions. He said nothing, but his pure heart was torn, Achilles saw, between their old deep affection for one another, which till now had been beyond question, and a kind of doubt, of shame even. He sees my indifference to the fate of these Greeks as a stain to my honour, Achilles told himself, and to his own.

He knew every movement of Patroclus' soul – how could he not after so long? – but would not allow himself to be swayed.

Patroclus had appeared at last in the hut and positioned himself, grim-faced and silently distraught, on a stool close to the entrance where his presence could not be ignored. There he waited.

Achilles, full of resentment at being judged, even in silence, and called to account, went on busying himself with nothing. Every moment of disunity between them was a torment to him. His quarrel with Agamemnon was a just one, his pride was touched. Did he have to argue that again? Agamemnon, because he was by nature vain and contentious, or because he had all along envied the ascendancy among them of a younger man, had openly insulted him.

The generals had awarded him as a prize of war a captured slave-girl, Briseis, and in the time she had been with him he had grown fond of her. Then Agamemnon's own prize, Chryseis, was ransomed and sent back to Troy, and the great commander, in his lordly way, had claimed *his* prize, Briseis, in her place. He had refused of course and not politely. And when Agamemnon, incensed at the rebuff, had roared and raged and crudely berated him, he too lost his temper and, barely able to restrain himself from striking the man, had stormed out of the assembly, retired to his hut, refused all further contact and withdrawn his troops from the battle-lines.

If the Greek generals were suffering now they had only themselves to blame. He and all his followers, including Patroclus, and his father Peleus, and their homeland Phthia, had been subjected to outrageous affront.

Of course he knew only too well what Patroclus intended by his brooding presence, and had for a long time endured it; but unused, where Patroclus was concerned, to holding in what he felt, had let angry disappointment at last get the better of him.

'If all this touches you so deeply, Patroclus,' he had flashed out, '*you* go and save the Greeks.'

17

'I will, since the great Achilles won't do it,' Patroclus hit back. And hand on sword he sprang to his feet. There were tears in his eyes.

They had stood then, appalled, both, by what had been said. Achilles was trembling; too proud to admit, even to this man who was half himself, that he might be in the wrong, but heartsick, stricken. When had they last quarrelled like this, he and Patroclus? When had he last seen Patroclus weep? The tears, he knew, were for him, he felt the hotness of them in his own throat. Even more for this unhappy rift between them.

'Patroclus,' he had whispered, and turned away.

'Achilles, let me go,' Patroclus begged, whispering himself now, though there were no others by. 'Let me go and take the Myrmidons with me. Lend me your armour. When the Trojans see your helmet and shield they will think it is Achilles who has returned to the field, and draw back and give our friends a breathing space. Achilles, I beg you.'

Filled with misgiving but suddenly drained of all will, Achilles had found himself assenting. When Patroclus, after so many days of tension, in a burst of joyful reconcilement clasped him to his breast, he had been convinced for a moment that all might be as Patroclus suggested, and could be turned about and made good. And when Patroclus, armed but not yet helmeted, himself again though the armour was not his, stood smiling before him, he too had smiled, though the feeling he caught from his dear friend's glowing freshness, the assurance and high spirits of the warrior armed for battle, did not last.

Alone in the hut again, feverish, drawn in upon himself, and with a heaviness like waking sleep upon him, he heard a shout go up from the assembled Greeks: his name – 'Achilles!' – then its echo from the Trojan lines, a hollow murmur like a rising wind.

Feeling hollow himself, as if his packed chest and limbs were without substance, he had got to his feet, and reeling a little, stepped outside to observe for himself what was under way.

Out there on the glittering plain, a figure dressed like him and moving as he did, resplendent in his harness, breastplate and greaves and holding aloft his studded shield, was standing alone between the lines. When the Greeks for a second time shouted his name, the figure turned in acknowledgement. His right arm jerked and hoisted aloft the flashing shield.

There was a rush, a great noise of raucous breath and clashing metal. Swords, heads, shoulders everywhere. 'Patroclus!' he had shouted, but silently, his cry snuffed out in the far-off spaces of his skull by the clangorous ringing of bronze against hammered bronze, as the helmet with the horsehair crest and nodding plume – *his* helmet, which every man at Troy, Greek and Trojan, recognised as his and knew him by – at a sudden swing as from nowhere (the gods again, their second thrust!) was struck from his head, and Patroclus, open-mouthed with astonishment, stepped back a pace, then staggered and went crashing.

He had wept for Patroclus. Wept without restraint. Sitting cross-legged on the ground, rocking back and forth in his anguish, pouring fistfuls of dust over his head.

Two days later, looking exactly as he had in life, the ghost of Patroclus had come to where he lay apart from the others, curled up like a child on the open beach on rounded stones that smelled of his mother, dry-damp seagrass. Over the long-drawn-out sobbing of the waves, Patroclus had begged him, in his old voice, tenderly, to cease calling so piteously upon him, to bury his body with all proper ceremony, but quickly, and to let his spirit go at last and make its way among the dead; and from that night on, Patroclus, for all his lying sleepless on his pallet, and watching, and waiting – though he restrains himself from calling – has not come back.

His bones now, the twelve long bones, the burnt-out brainpan, the handful of splintered fragments they had gathered from the ashes of his pyre, are in the wide-mouthed urn in the barrow Achilles has raised to his dear friend's memory. Where in time his own will join them.

'Just a little longer, Patroclus,' he whispers. 'Can you hear me? Soon, now. Soon.'

But first he had Patroclus' killer to deal with, in a last encounter out there under the walls of Troy.

The armour Hector wore was the armour he had stripped from the body of Patroclus, Achilles' own, which Hector wore now to mock him: the helmet with its horsehair crest and plumes, the bronze harness that hung from his shoulders, the greaves with their silver clasps at ankle and knee.

Confronting an enemy so armed, at close quarters, sword to sword at the end of an hour-long pursuit, dodging this way and that to anticipate or avoid the other's thrusts, searching out, as he knew it from within, the one unprotected place in the corselet – at the gullet, where the collarbone yields to the soft flesh of the neck – was like trying to deceive or outguess his shadow, and aiming, beyond Hector, at himself. And Hector's death when it came, in *his* armour, like watching for a second time the dreamlike enactment of his own.

He dodged and feinted, found the place, and grim-faced but secretly smiling eased the heavy weapon in.

Hector, eyes wide with disbelief, dropped his sword, reached out and closed his fist on Achilles' own. With the hot sweat streaming from his brow, every muscle in his forearm knotted in a last act of defiance, he met Achilles' gaze.

Achilles grunted, gave the sword another push. The whole weight of his body hung on the thrust.

Weightless himself. All the force of his brute pres-ence gone now into the blade as he urged it in. There was a still, extended moment when they were joined, he and Hector, by three hand-spans of tempered bronze.

On his knees in the dust, Hector gazed up at him, his grip still locked on Achilles' fist. And despite the death-wound he had received, in a spirit untouched by the old rancour, with an almost brotherly concern, he spoke to Achilles with the last of his breath; as men, both, for whom this moment was sacred; a meeting that from the begin-ning had been the clear goal of their lives and the final achievement of what they were. Man to man, but impersonally. So that Achilles, leaning close, felt a shiver go through him as he recognised the precise point where Hector's own breath gave out and what replaced it was the voice of a god.

'You will not long outlive me, Achilles,' the voice whispered. Then, 'The days are few now that you have to walk on the earth. To eat and exchange talk with your companions and enjoy the pleasures of women. Already, away there in your father's house in Phthia, they are preparing to mourn.'

Achilles, leaning in over his sword to catch the

last of Hector's breath, felt the big body sway a moment, then stagger. Brought down by its own weight, blood gushing from the soft place between neck and clavicle, it detached itself from the blade and rolled slowly back.

Achilles too staggered a moment. He felt his soul change colour. Blood pooled at his feet, and though he continued to stand upright and triumphant in the sun, his spirit set off on its own downward path and approached the borders of an unknown region. For the length of a heartbeat it hesitated, then went on.

How long he passed in that twilit kingdom he would never know. It was another, more obdurate self that found its way back; and stood unmoved, unmoving, as his Myrmidons formed a cordon round Hector's corpse and stripped it of its armour – harness, corselet, greaves – till all it was left with was the short tunic, now soiled with sweat and torn and drenched with blood, that was Hector's own. Then he stood watching again as one by one, without passion, but also without pity, they plunged their swords into Hector's unprotected flesh; with each blow shouting his name, so that all those watching from the walls of Troy would hear it, and Hector too, wherever he might be on his downward path into the underworld, would hear it and look mournfully back.

Achilles watched. Himself like a dead man. Feeling nothing.

When they were done and had stepped away, he roused himself and approached the body. Stood staring down at it. Then, taking a knife from his belt, he fell to one knee, and swiftly, as if he had always known that this was what he would do, slashed one after the other from ankle to heel the tendons of Hector's feet.

His men looked on. They could not imagine what he was up to.

Unwinding from his waist an oxhide thong, he lifted the feet and lashed them together; then, with the thong wound tight around his wrist, dragged the corpse to his chariot. Passing the thong once, twice, three times round the beechwood axlebar, he made it fast to the car. Jerked the hide to see that it would hold. Then, like a man obeying the needs of some other, darker agency, he leapt onto the platform, dashed the stinging sweat-drops from his eyes, touched the horses lightly with the traces and wheeled out onto the plain, half-turning from time to time to observe how the body, its head and shoulders bouncing over the dry uneven ground, swung in a wide arc behind him.

They were moving slowly as yet. The horses, excited by his presence and the promise of exercise, jerked their heads.

Leaning forward, he whispered to them, dark syllables of horse magic, then loosed the reins.

Behind him the body, its locks already grey with dust, leapt and followed, the hip-bones and the shoulderblades of the massive back dashing hard against sharp-edged flinty stones and ridges as, time after time with gathering speed, the wheels of the light car took to the air, then struck down hard again in a shower of sparks. Faster and faster he drove, up and down under the walls of Troy, his hair loose and flying, gouts of sweat flung from his brow, as Hector's corpse, raw now from head to foot and caked with dust, bounded and tumbled, and Priam, Hector's father, and his mother Hecuba, and his wife Andromache with the child Astyanax at her hip, and Hector's brothers and brothers-in-law and their wives, and all the common people of Troy, who had flocked to every vantage point on the walls, looked on.

Still he felt nothing. Only the tautness of the muscles in his forearm where all the veins were puffed and thickened, and in his toes where they gripped the platform of the car. Only the humming of the air, and its scorching touch as it eddied round and past him.

He was waiting for the rage to fill him that would be equal at last to the outrage he was committing. That would assuage his grief, and be so convincing to the witnesses of this barbaric spectacle that he too might believe there was a living man at the centre of it, and that man himself.

In full sunlight now, face taut and wind-chopped, the skin over his cheekbones stiff with salt, salt on his dry lips when he wets them, Achilles comes to the outskirts of the camp.

All is activity here, the day has begun. From off in the distance a lowing of cattle, a bleating of sheep crowded close in their pens. In the stillness somewhere, the knock of an axe.

But the sun has not yet reached the encampment. A powdering of frost whitens the base of the pine-trunks that make up the high stockade wall. Small fires are burning, most of them no more now than embers, sending up thin trails of smoke. The guards who crouch beside them, or stride up and down flapping their arms in the morning chill, are wakeful but sleepy-eyed at the end of their watch.

They are men from his home country, clear-spirited and secure in their animal nature, un-acquainted with second thoughts. Their sinewy limbs and hard-bitten features, like his own, come from tramping the craggy uplands that in summer, when hawks hang on updraughts over the granite peaks, are ablaze with a compacted heat that invests the whole upper air with its fiery intensity, and in winter become tracts of ice. Their fathers are smallholders who raise wheat in the deep soil of the flatlands and grow small sweet grapes on the ridges above; keep herds of long-horned cattle, and sheep whose milk goes into the curds their women make. On their tongues, as on his, the harsh north-country dialect, full of insults that are also backhanded terms of affection. Its wry jokes and weather-rhymes are the proof in their mouths of a link between them that is older than the oaths of loyalty they swear.

They have the minds of hawks, these men, of foxes and of the wolves that come at night to the snowy folds and are tracked and hunted. They love him. He has long since won their love. It is unconditional.

But when they look at him these days, what they see confounds them. They no longer know what authority they are under. He is their leader, but he breaks daily every rule they have been taught to live by. Their only explanation is that he is mad. That some rough-haired god has darkened his mind and moves now like an opposing stranger in him, occupying the place where reason and rule should be, and sleep, and honour of other men and the gods.

He makes his way past them, and on to where his horses are kept, and the fast light chariot where Patroclus once stood beside him is housed in its shed. He calls up his grooms. Orders them, as he has each morning now for eleven days, to lead out his horses, wheel out his chariot and make all ready for use.

The men obey, but they know what he has in mind and cannot bear to meet his eye.

He watches them work, striding impatiently up and down the yard. On the lookout for some fault he may find with them. Inwardly raging.

But they know how he is these mornings and take care. When the horses come trotting out they are combed and glossy, the spokes and felloes of the chariot wheels have been sponged clean, the rails of the car freshly burnished. They have done their work well. He is punctilious, but so are they. Let him rage as he will and do his looking.

They smile at one another, but show nothing when, after walking twice around the car and stopping half a dozen times to scrutinise their work, he nods and turns to the horses.

These horses were a gift from the gods at his parents' wedding. Balius and Xanthus, they are called. He whispers a word or two in their ear that the grooms do not catch, and they lift their heads, shake their oiled manes, their dark coats rippling. Though they have a divine spark and are immortal, they are also creatures like any other, and so sensitive in their animal nature, so responsive to every shift of their master's thought, that they seem endowed with a reason and sympathy that is almost human.

Xanthus, the more nervous, the more impulsive of the two, is Achilles' favourite. He lays his hand now, very gently, on the satiny hide; senses the lightning quiver of muscle under the almost transparent skin. Leaning close to the leathery soft lip, and feeling warm breath on his cheek, he experiences a rush of tenderness that might be for himself; of awe too at the other life of this magic being; and when he observes the eyes of the grooms upon him with their question – What's he up to now? – a kind of envy for how free the creature is of a self-consciousness that at times makes us strange to ourselves and darkly divided.

He gives Xanthus a hearty thwack on the rump, then, leaping nimbly into the car, drives slowly to where Hector's corpse, the feet still lashed together, the arms outflung, lies tumbled in the dirt. No need to get down. He can see from where he stands that all is as it was yesterday, and the day before, and as it has been each day since the beginning. The gods continue to defy him.

Hector lies as if sleeping. His features are those of a young bridegroom newly refreshed, his locks glossy-black as in life, the brow like marble, all the welts and gashes where yesterday bone showed through smoothly sealed and the torn flesh made whole again.

Half-blind with rage, Achilles jumps down from the car, hoists the corpse by its feet to the axlebar, and with a brutal swiftness loops the thong three times round the bar, jerks it firm, then savagely knots it. He is dealing with a sack of bones. As the dogs know, who yelp and howl at having been kept so long from what they would tear at.

'Later,' their keeper whispers as, crouched beside them and holding fast to their leads, he watches Achilles at his task. 'Later, my loves,' he tells them. 'When *he* is finished with it.'

Achilles has remounted the car. A trail of dust billows behind him as he drives out across the plain. Ahead, the barrow with the bones of Patroclus, marking the spot where he had erected the pyre, a hundred feet long, a hundred feet wide, where Patroclus was burned.

Fat sheep and cattle had been slaughtered round the base. He himself had cut gobbets of fat from the carcasses and covered the body with them; laid precious two-handled jars filled with oil and honey against the bier, and cast four splendid horses on the pyre that screamed and shook fire from their coats when their throats were slashed. He had cut the throats as well of two of the nine dogs Patroclus kept, and dragged a dozen highborn Trojan prisoners to the place, all the time raging and weeping. And still it was not enough. Still his grief was not consumed.

All that great pile of offerings is gone now over the plain, as smuts and scattered ashes. Only the barrow remains, and the urn with his dear friend's bones.

Achilles slows as he approaches it. The horses lift their feet in a ceremonial trot, the wheels of the chariot barely turning.

From the platform of the car, hawk-faced and grim, Achilles looks down. The tears he brings fall inwardly, his cheeks are dry. He glances back over his shoulder to where Hector lies face-down in the dust. All this, he tells himself, is for you, Patroclus.

But it is never enough. That is what he feels. That is what torments him.

With a jerk of the reins he pulls the horses to the left, and with a great shout sets them off at a furious pace to gallop once, twice, three times round the barrow, the body of Hector, as it tumbles behind, raising a dust cloud that swirls and thickens as if at that spot on the plain a storm had gathered and for long minutes raged and twisted while all around it the world remained still.

In the yard a thousand paces off, the grooms stand with shaded eyes, watching. The guards pause in their tasks around the camp.

Higher and higher the column climbs, spreading its branches. Then it stills, hangs, and comes sifting down in shadowy streaks like distant rain.

Achilles is driving back now. Leaden-limbed, covered from head to toe in dust. Grey-headed with it. His face, arms, clothes, hands caked with it. Like a man who has climbed out of his grave.

He is as fouled with dust as the thing – bloody and unrecognisable – that he trails from his axle-bar.

Tired now, his wrists like water, he drives to where the grooms wait in the yard.

It offends them, though they dare not show it, that he should bring back horses that just minutes ago went out glossy and sprightly on their feet, all ghostly grey and foaming.

He climbs down from the car. Says nothing as he throws the reins to the first man who comes running.

He will sleep now. Too tired even to wash, he goes immediately to his hut, rolls up in his cloak on a pallet in the corner and within seconds is drowned in oblivion.

Swiftness of foot is his special distinction among the Greeks: Achilles the Runner. The quickness of his spirit to haul air into his lungs, to feed their overplus of energy and lightness to his foot soles and heels, to the muscles of his calves, the long tendons of his thighs, is an animal quality he shares with the wolves of his native uplands, bodies elongated, fur laid flat as they run under the wind.

His runner spirit has deserted him. It is the earth-heaviness in him of all his organs, beginning with the heart, that he must throw off if he is to be himself again.

He is waiting for the break. For something to appear that will break the spell that is on him, the self-consuming rage that drives him and wastes his spirit in despair. Something new and unimaginable as yet that will confront him with the need, in meeting it, to leap clear of the clogging grey web that enfolds him.

Meanwhile, day after day, he rages, shames himself, calls silently on a spirit that does not answer, and sleeps.

Laid out on uneven ground along a rocky bluff,
Troy is a city of four-square towers topped by
untidy storks' nests, each as tall as a man; of dove-
cotes, cisterns, yards where black goats are penned,
and in a maze of cobbled squares and alleys, houses
of whitewashed mud-brick and stone, cube-shaped
and with open stairways that at this hour mount to
dreams. On the flat roofs under awnings of woven
rush, potted shrubs spread their heavy night
odours, and cats, of the haughty small-skulled
breed that are native to the region, prowl the para-
pets and yowl like tormented souls in their mating.
Tucked in between rocky outcrops there are kitchen
gardens, with a fig tree, a pomegranate, a row or

two of lettuce or broad beans, a clump of herbs where snails the size of a baby's fingernail are reborn in their dozens after a storm and hang like raindrops from every stalk.

Here for eleven nights another man has been wrestling with dark thoughts as he lies sleepless on his couch – but sleepless in his case, like so much else in his life, is a manner of speaking. It is what he feels is proper to his grief.

In fact he has slept, but so fitfully, picking his way past eddies of murky flame, and corpses heaped in piles round fallen archways or crammed into wells, that when he wakes it is to a deeper exhaustion.

The grief that racks him is not only for his son Hector. It is also for a kingdom ravaged and threatened with extinction, for his wife, Hecuba, and the many sons and daughters and their children who stand under his weak protection; and for Troy, once a place of refinement and of ceremonies pleasing to the gods, now, in the waking dreams that night after night trouble his rest, a burnt-out shell, whose citizens – though they believe themselves quietly asleep and safe in their beds – are the corpses he moves among: headless, limbless,

40

savagely hacked, hovered about by ghostly exhalations and the fires of the dead. Flies cluster at their nostrils and the corners of their eyes. Dogs lick up the spatter of their brains, gnaw at their shoulder-bones and skulls and on the small bones of their feet. Above, among towering smoke trails, birds of prey hang waiting for the dogs to be done.

Priam groans, and the chamber servant on his cot at the entrance starts awake. 'No, no,' he calls, but weakly. 'It is nothing. There's nothing I need.'

The servant settles. The room falls still.

But something now is different. The air, as in the wake of some other, less physical disturbance, shimmers with a teasing iridescence.

Priam comes to attention. He knows from long experience what is expected of him. Stays ready but still.

Often, in the lapse of light in the chamber where he sits nodding, or in a leisure hour beside the fish-pond in his garden, one or other of the gods will materialise, jelly-like, out of the radiant vacancy. An old, dreamlike passivity in him that he no longer finds it necessary to resist will dissolve the boundary between what is solid and tangible in the world around him – mulberry leaves afloat on their shadows, the knobbly extrusions on the trunk of a pine – and the weightless medium in which his consciousness is adrift, where the gods, in their bodily presence, have the same consistency as his thoughts.

Two of his children, his daughter Cassandra and the high priest Helenus, have inherited his powers, but in a form that sets a question against them. For all his reverence – he might say as a necessary part of it – he is wary in his dealings with the gods, who do not always act openly, or so he has discovered. He treads lightly in their presence.

Cassandra, enraptured and pure, has none of his pious trepidation. Poor child! Her brothers taunt her without mercy, seeing in this half-crazed mystic and self-proclaimed bride of Apollo a girl who has always claimed too much for herself, a practised attention-seeker – and Priam is inclined to agree, but is too fond of the child to speak openly against her. Intoxicated, overwrought, in service to a deity who takes her physically, or so she believes, in a swathe of flame, she alarms her father with the hot thoughts her god has breathed into her mouth, some of which, however terrible he finds them, he cannot wholly dismiss.

Helenus, by contrast, is Apollo's consecrated priest. What exists quite naturally in Priam as an aspect of daily being, and in Cassandra as self-induced hysteria, has in Helenus taken a sleek professional form. Austere and commanding but entirely conventional, he is a man, Priam feels, who is too comfortable in the flesh.

Only in Priam has what is both a blessing and an awful responsibility remained close to the source. His nature is open at any moment to presences in the air around him that, when they settle out and take a bodily form, have the names of gods.

So it is now. Seated on the edge of his couch, what Priam catches out of the corner of his eye is the hem of a vanishing garment, and on the air the last breath of a message he has now to fix his mind on and recall.

He is obliged, in his role as king, to think of the king's sacred body, this brief six feet of earth he moves and breathes in – aches and sneezes and all – as at once a body like any other and an abstract of the lands he represents, their living map.

Holding in his head all the roads that lead out to the distant parts of his kingdom, he feels them at times as ribbons tied at the centre of him, for the most part loose but sometimes stretched taut and pulling a little, according to what is occurring out there – events that his body is aware of as a dim foreboding long before the last in a relay of messengers, who for days have been running down dusty roads, bursts in to deliver it as news.

He has, two or three times during his reign, gone with a train of companions on a progress through his far-flung territories. To show himself, and to see a little of what it is out there that he represents. But his more usual role is to stand still at the centre, both actual and symbolic in the same breath, and to experience those dual states quite naturally as one.

As now, when from high up in the coffered ceiling of his chamber he catches an echo of what in other circumstances might be words.

After eleven days of watching and silent prayer, in which no food and not a drop of wine has passed his lips, a response!

His son Hector had fallen before his eyes. From a bastion at the highest point of the city walls he had looked on helpless as Achilles, working quickly, like a man under instruction from his daemon or following the contours of a dream, dragged the corpse to his car, secured it, knot after knot, to the axle-tree, and hauled it off through the tumbling dust.

Half-mad with grief he had broken from the scene and rushed down to the Scaean Gates – meaning to do what? he hardly knew. And when Pammon and Helenus caught up with him and drew him back, had sunk down in the dirt and straw of the public street, and with howls that in their pain and desolation must have seemed bearlike fouled his head with excrement, that filth his crown – his only crown now as the gods clearly intended, so that when they looked down, those high ones, they would see with no possibility of disguise what they had accomplished: this ancient doll they had set up, and for so long prized and flattered, reduced once more to what he had been when they first reached down and plucked him out, an abandoned child, all grimed and stinking; a child now with seventy years on his back, and all that lies between, the extravagant pageant of his days as Priam, King of Troy, a mockery as they had all along intended.

'No, Priam, you are wrong.'

He starts, and when he turns and looks his eyes dazzle.

Seated close by him on the couch is the goddess Iris. She is smiling. Indulgently, he thinks. The soft light she appears in has a calming effect, and his heart opens to what she whispers in his ear.

'Not a mockery, my friend, but the way things *are*. Not the way they must be, but the way they have turned out. In a world that is also subject to chance.'

'Chance?'

He has spoken the word aloud. Again the servant stirs. Priam turns quickly to the place, afraid that if the fellow wakes and calls, the dreamlike spell that is on him may be broken.

And in fact, when he turns back, though her words continue to drop directly into his thoughts, the goddess is gone. Only the last of her shining is on the room, and he wonders – he is by nature doubtful – if even this is only an after-effect of his waking.

But where else could such a dangerous suggestion come from if not from an immortal? One of those who are free to raise blasphemous questions, because in being just that, immortal, they will never be subject to what might follow from the answer.

Chance?

Bewildered, but also strangely excited, he sets his feet to the pavement and feels about for his slippers.

His mind is as clear now as if he had slept for the whole of these eleven days and nights and woken entirely restored, his spirits quickened and lightly expanding in him.

He sits very still, his shoulders in the spare frame a little sunken; and the picture that forms before him is of himself seated just as he is here, but in full sunlight on the crossbench of a cart. A plain wooden cart, of the kind that workmen use for carrying firewood or hay, and drawn by two coal-black mules.

He himself is dressed in a plain white robe without ornament. No jewelled amulet at his breast. No golden armbands or any other form of royal insignia.

On the bench beside him the driver of the cart is a man, not so old as himself but not young either. A bull-shouldered fellow he has never seen before, in an ungirdled robe of homespun. A bearded, shaggy-headed fellow, rough but not fearsome.

Behind them, the bed of the wagon is covered

with a wicker canopy, and something there is shining out from under a plain white cover. Gold or bronze it must be. It is pouring out light.

But he knows what it is – no need to lift a corner of the cloth and look beneath.

Quickly he rises, and passing the servant, who this time does not stir, swings open the door to his chamber and begins down the corridor. 'Hecuba,' he mutters. His blood is racing. This good news is for Hecuba, though he fears already – his doubting nature again – what her response will be when she hears his plan.

Outside, the corridor is dark, save for braziers set at easy arm's reach along the wall and extending at intervals to the distant portal. The effect is of a black flood that has risen above head height, thick, solemn, lapping at the flickering redness of the upper walls, so that stepping out into it, what he feels is an unaccustomed lack of ease – he for whose convenience everything here is arranged by the conscientious forethought of stewards and the labour of a hundred slaves.

Here and there, as he passes, the faces of servants who sit backs to the wall, at this or that chamber entrance, loom up in the dark. Startled to see him at this hour and unattended, they stir and mutter the usual courtesies, but he is gone before they can stumble to their feet.

Yes, yes, he thinks, all this I know is unprecedented.

But so is his plan. This plunging at near dawn down a deserted corridor is just the beginning. He will get used to the unaccustomed. It is what he is after.

He feels bold now, defiant. Sure of his decision.

If he is to face Hecuba and prevail, he has to be.

He finds her already risen and sitting, very erect, on the day bed in her sitting room. A cruse lamp is burning at the top of a tall copper stand. At her feet a pot of embers – she suffers from the cold – throws out a feeble warmth.

She too has not slept. Her hair is awry – that is what he sees first. But as soon as she catches sight of him, with her old pride in her beauty, and the wish as always to appear at her best before him, her hand, in a gesture that like everything she does is precise, controlled, with its own practical elegance, goes to the bodkin that holds it, and in a moment all is restored.

He watches, says nothing. Moved again by the tenderness they have so long shared, he seats himself beside her and takes her hand. It is no longer white now but veined and mottled like his own with liver-coloured spots, the flesh between the fine bones, which his fingertips gently feel for, puckered and slack. He raises it to his lips, and she casts a piteous look upon him. Her eyelids are swollen with tears.

'Hecuba. My dear,' he whispers, and she allows herself, almost girlishly, to be held and comforted.

They sit a moment, holding one another like children. The lamp flickers. She weeps. When her tears have come to an end, and she has once again taken control of herself, he begins.

'My dear,' he says softly, 'it is eleven days now since Hector's death and we have done nothing, all of us, but weep and sit stunned with grief. I know *I* have wept, and I see from this that you are still full of tears. And how could we do less, any one of us, for such a son and brother, such a fearless protector of Troy and its people? And you most of all, my dear, who have lost so many sons in these last terrible years.'

He has much to tell her and wants to lead up to it slowly. He wants her to see the plan he is about to lay before her not as something desperate and wild but as the result on his part – though it is not, of course – of consideration and careful thought.

But the look she casts upon him is so fierce that he draws back and cannot go on. He feels the hard purpose he has come with flutter in him and fail.

'Tears,' she mutters, almost to herself. 'Oh, I have plenty of those. But not of grief. Of anger, fury, that I am a woman and can do nothing but sit here and rage and weep while the body of my son Hector, after eleven days and nights, is still out there on the plain, unwashed, unanointed, and eleven times now their noble Achilles has dragged him up and down before the Greek ships – my son, my dear son Hector! – and tumbled his poor head in the dirt. Oh, if I could get my hands on that butcher I'd tear his heart out and eat it raw!'

Priam quails before this small, fierce, straight-backed woman he has known and not known for so many years.

'I carried him,' she whispers, 'here, here,' and

her clenched fist beats at the hollow under her heart. 'It is *my* flesh that is being tumbled on the stones out there. Seven times now I've grieved for a son lost in this war. And what I remember of each one is how they kicked their little heels under my heart – here, just here – and the first cry they gave when I yielded them up to the world, and the first steps they took. Troilus was very late in walking – do you recall that, Priam? You used to tempt him with a little dagger you had, with a dog's head on the handle – do you recall that?' – and she searches his face for a response. 'I was in labour for eighteen hours with Hector. That is what I recall when I think of his body being tumbled over the stones and left out there for dogs to tear at and maul.'

Priam shakes his head. This kind of women's talk unnerves him. It is not in his sphere. He remembers nothing of a dagger carved like a dog, or that his son Troilus had been slow to walk. What he recalls is a series of small squalling bundles, each one presented to him like a bloodied human offering on the outstretched palms of an attendant. To be recognised as his, and blessed and gathered into his household. What he recalls is that Troilus is dead, like so many of his sons. Like Hector. This talk of dogs' heads and daggers has diverted him from what he has come to tell her and makes it difficult for him to begin. But after a moment of quiet restraint he does so.

'Hecuba,' he ventures. 'After all this time, these eleven days of doing nothing but weep and think and think again, I have come to a decision – no, no, let me finish, you can make your objections, I know you will have objections, afterwards, when I've had my say.

'I am too old, I know, to put on armour and go to the field. To ride into the fray and leap down from my chariot and crack heads, and sweat and get bloody. And the truth is I never was a warrior, it was not my role. My role was to hold myself apart in ceremonial stillness and let others be my arm, my fist – my breath too when talk was needed, because outside my life here in the court and with you, my dear, where I do like to speak a little, I have always had a herald at my side, our good Idaeus, to find words for me. To be seen as a man like other men – human as we are, all of us – would have suggested that I was impermanent and weak. Better to stand still and keep silent, so that when old age came upon me, as it has at last, the world would not see how shaky my grip has become, and how cracked and thin my voice. Only that I am still here. Fixed and permanent. Unchangeable, therefore unchanged. Well, you know I am changed, my dear, because from you nothing of what I am, or almost nothing, is hidden. To others I am what I have always been – great Priam. But only because they have never really looked at me. And when they do look, what they see is what they are meant to see. The fixed mark to which everything else in my kingdom refers. A ceremonial figurehead that might just as well be of stone or wood. So – to come at last to what I want to tell you.

'This morning, as I was sitting quietly on my couch just after waking, a vision came to me. Not quite a dream,' and taking a good breath he begins to paint for Hecuba how he had seen himself seated in a wagon drawn by two black mules, plainly dressed in a white robe and with none of the signs of kingship upon him, no amulet, no armband or any other sort of regalia; and just recalling it now, allowing the lines of the picture to grow clear as he adds one detail then the next, makes him more certain than ever that what he intends to do is what he must do.

But to Hecuba the image is a shocking one – she is more tied to convention than she believes – and as Priam warms to his subject she grows more and more disturbed.

What Priam is speaking of is a dream. Dreams are subtle, shifting, they are meant to be read, not taken literally. Hidden away in what they appear to present are signs that must be seized on by a mind that can see past mere actualities to what hovers luminously beyond. She has spent all the years of their marriage dealing with these visions that afflict him. She prepares now to reply as she normally would, but Priam prevents her.

'No, no, my dear,' he insists, 'I am not finished,' and the firmness of this, which is unusual, makes her pause. He goes on quickly to describe the driver who sits beside him on the bench, the wicker-work canopy over the bed of the wagon, the load they are carrying.

'It shines out,' he whispers, his voice touched with wonder as if the wagon were actually there in the room with them, 'from under a plain white coverlet. And though I cannot see it –' he blinks, he is very aware of her stopped breath – 'though I cannot see it, I know what it is. It is the better part of my treasury. Gold coins, armour and arms, plate, tripods, cauldrons, the rare gold cup – my favourite, you know the one, that the Thracians gave me all those years ago when I went on an embassy to them – all shining out as I sit on the bench beside the driver and we travel on under the night.

'Then, my dear,' and his voice quickens, 'it is no longer night. And this time, when I look behind me, what is glowing out from under the coverlet, under the wickerwork canopy, is the body of my son Hector, all his limbs newly restored and shining, restored and *ransomed*. And that is it,' he whispers before she can protest out of the stricken face she has turned upon him, 'that is what I intend to do. To go today, immediately, to Achilles, just as I saw myself in my dream, plainly dressed and with no attendant but a driver for the cart – not as a king but as an ordinary man, a father, and offer him a ransom, and in the sight of the gods, who must surely look down in pity on me, beg him humbly, on my knees if that is what it comes to, to give me back the body of my son.'

His voice breaks and he turns quickly away. He dares not meet her look. When he does at last, Hecuba, her eyes narrowed, is still staring at him.

She nods her head. Rapidly. She is, he knows, controlling herself. He must be strong now. He has always been afraid of this controlled rage in her.

'And you expect him to do it?' she hisses. The scorn in her voice is withering. 'You expect that . . . jackal, that noble bully, to be moved by this touching pantomime?'

She gets up and begins to stride about. The lamp flickers in the air she stirs up, as, small, straight, furious, she passes back and forth before him.

'When Hector accepted Achilles' challenge and very courteously offered him terms of combat – to allow no insult to Achilles' body if he prevailed but to give it over, in the time-honoured way, to be dealt with as the gods demand – what did the man do? He rejected the offer with contempt, and when Hector –' she paused, unable to speak the word – 'when victory went to the Greek, he let his henchmen loose on my dear son's body, and twenty times over, one after another, they plunged their daggers into his flesh. Why? For what reason? To vent their spite on him, the cowards, for being what Achilles will never be, a man with no blemish on his soul, shining pure before the gods. He tied Hector's feet to the axlebar of his chariot, a thing unheard of, and dragged his body in the dust. And you expect this wolf, this violator of every law of gods and men, to take the gift you hold out to him and act like a *man*?'

'I do not expect it,' Priam says quietly. 'I believe it is possible. I believe –' and he is astonished at the enormity of the thought he is expressing, he whose whole life has been guided by what is established and conventional – surely, he thinks, it is a goddess who is speaking through me. 'I believe,' he says, 'that the thing that is needed to cut this knot we are all tied in is something that has never before been done or thought of. Something impossible. Something *new*.'

She composes herself, hoods her eyes and sits. The assurance with which he has spoken, the quietness that has spread around them, makes her wary: she must not cross him. But the danger of what he is determined on fills her with alarm. She will need all her wiles, all her powers of firm but calm persuasion, to lead him back from it.

'But you would never get there,' she whispers.

'Some swaggering lout among the Greeks would strike you down before you got even halfway to the camp. Think of it. Two old men in a cart laden with gold? Do you suppose your grey hairs would save you?'

'No,' he admits. 'But the gods might. If it was their intention that I get there.'

'Priam, Priam,' she sighs, and again takes his hand. 'This is folly.'

'It is, yes. I know. But what seems foolish is just what is most sensible sometimes. The fact that it has never been done, that it is novel, unthinkable – except that *I* have thought of it – is just what makes me believe it should be attempted. It is possible because it is not possible. And because it is simple. Why do we think always that the simple thing is beneath us? Because we are kings? What I do is what any man might do.'

'But you are not *any* man.'

'That's true. In one way I'm not. But in another, deeper way, I am. I feel a kind of freedom in that. It's a feeling I like, it appeals to me. And perhaps, because it is unexpected, it may appeal to him too: the chance to break free of the obligation of being always the hero, as I am expected always to be the king. To take on the lighter bond of being simply a man. Perhaps that is the real gift I have to bring him. Perhaps that is the ransom.'

Hecuba shakes her head. 'And if you too are lost? Who will stand by me in what we know is to come? Because we know, both of us, what that is, and can speak of it here where there is no one else to hear it. Just ourselves and the gods.'

Her voice has fallen to the merest breath. The flame of the lamp, too, gutters and falls.

'Who will share this weight of sorrow that is coming to us? And when my spirit fails, who will lend me the hand of comfort as you do now, my dear one? Who will keep Troy, our beloved city, alive with at least a semblance of the old neighbourliness and order if its great centre and source is gone?'

They sit in silence now, her hand in his. They have spoken of these things before. Quietly, soberly. They are two old people consulting together, seeking comfort in one another's presence. Two children holding hands in the dark.

'Am I being selfish?' she asks at length.

But the question is to herself and he has no answer. His voice too when he replies is no more than a breath.

'If I do not succeed in this, and am lost, then all is lost. We must leave that to the gods. Or to chance.'

There! – and a little shiver goes through him – he has said it.

Chance?

She looks up quickly. Surely she has misheard.

'It seems to me,' he says, almost dreamily, 'that there might be another way of naming what we call fortune and attribute to the will, or the whim, of the gods. Which offers a kind of opening. The opportunity to act for ourselves. To try something that might force events into a different course.'

She wishes she had misheard. Words are powerful. They too can be the agents of what is new, of what is conceivable and can be thought and let loose upon the world. That Priam of all men should say such things – he who has always been so observant of what is established and lawful – makes her wonder now if his wits are not unstrung. She needs time. She needs the help of her sons.

'Listen, my dear, this plan of yours, if you really mean to go through with it, should be put to our sons, to Helenus and the rest, in council. That is the proper course.' She allows herself a moment's pause. 'As for this other matter –' she cannot bring herself to use *his* word – 'this idea you're so taken with, of how and why things happen as they do, that is not to be spoken of. Imagine what it would lead to, what would be permitted. The randomness, the violence. Imagine the panic it would spread. You must, I beg you, keep that strictly to yourself. Now, I will go and give orders to have a fire set under the cauldron and water heated for your bath,' and she steps swiftly to the door and calls a servant. Priam meanwhile, dreamily absorbed, continues to sit upright on the edge of the bed. When she returns he is still sitting.

'My dear,' she says, 'what is it? What more?'

She is dry-eyed, intent, efficient. She has her own plan now to forestall him.

'Hecuba,' he begins, 'there is something else I want you to hear. Something that till now I have never spoken of in all the many intimate hours we have spent together. Even to you, my dear, who know all my doubts and foibles, and little shameful anxieties and fears. Not because I wanted to be secretive – you of all people know I am not – and anyway, you have your own sweet ways of getting around me, so what would be the use? I have not spoken of these things because I did not know how to. How even to begin.'

He shakes his head, slowly shakes it again, then, composing himself, takes Hecuba's small hand and holds it close to his breast. She responds with an answering pressure of her own. She is sensitive to the slightest shades in him, but he is odd today – she has no idea where all this is leading.

'You know my story,' he says softly. 'You must have heard it a hundred times as a child in your father's palace, away there in Phrygia, long before you knew that one day you would make the journey here and be my bride.' He smiles at this: the thought comforts him. It is a fact of such long standing, a story now in itself. 'I wonder what you thought of it, and of me. Perhaps even then your heart was touched, and what you felt then, as a mere girl, has led to this lifetime we have spent – very lovingly, I think – in one another's company.'

He raises her hand to his lips, meeting her concentrated, soft-eyed gaze, and glimpsing in it, as from afar, the child he has just evoked: frowning, half-fearful, hanging on the story at whose midpoint his own small life was suspended.

'Well, it's a tale every child knows and has heard

a hundred times over, from his nurse at bedtime or from some weaver of magic in the marketplace. The beginning. The long-drawn-out and terrifying business of its middle. Then all in an instant – in what is always a surprise, even when the listener knows already what is to come – the turnabout, the happy end. However often he may have heard it the listener sits breathless, his small soul hanging on a breath. In just a moment a miracle will occur, and the little victim, the lost one – me in this case – will be snatched up and happily restored.

'Imagine, then, what it was like to *be* that child. To actually stand as I did at the centre of it, of what was not a story, not yet, but a real happening, all noise and smoke and panicky confusion. To know nothing of what is to come and simply *be there* – one of a horde of wailing infants, some no more than three or four years old, who have been driven like geese out of the blazing citadel, along with rats, mice and a dozen other small, terrified creatures, all squealing underfoot. A rabble of filthy, lice-ridden brats with the mark of the whip across their shoulders, the spawn of beggars, pedlars, scullery maids, stablehands, whores. And smuggled in among them, whimpering and pale, a few little pampered lords such as I was, who'd seen their parents slaughtered, and their brothers laid out with their white throats slashed. All hiding now – smeared with shit to disguise the scent of sweet herbs on their skin – among all those others. Utterly bewildered like them, and waiting, too tired and hungry to be properly afraid, for some bully to come swaggering up, all matted hair and sweat, who has grown tired of slitting bellies and smashing skulls and is ready now for a little harmless fun. Ready to amuse himself by poking ribs, and pushing his thick finger into a mouth, and carrying off this or that one of us to be his slave and plaything, his prize of war.

'We huddle in groups, half-asleep on our feet. The air's an oven thick with smoke. It's past midday. Since the slaughter began, just after dawn, not a drop of water has passed our lips.

'Some of the smallest among us are blubbering snot and crying for their mothers. Others are too stunned to do more than squat in their own filth. We cling together, all grimed with ashes and streaked with the dried blood of whoever it was, a parent or some kindly neighbour, whose arms we were snatched from. Waiting in the open now for the men whose voices we can hear, in a great roar up there in the city, to descend like wolves and carry us off.

'A group of guards has been set to watch us. They are idle fellows, some of them bloodied and in bandages, all of them terrifying to a child who has never known any but men whose every move is a response to the fulfilling of his needs. Their rough voices, their hands, their red mouths scare me. They range round the edges of the crowd, pushing and shouting. Even more frightful, when they produce them, are their grins.

'Occasionally, out of boredom, or the need for a moment's savage amusement, they toss handfuls of crusts into the crowd, and laugh as the boldest or most desperate of the mob of hungry, half-naked urchins fall upon them, scrabbling in the dirt and lashing out with knuckles and bare feet, howling, biting, gouging. The men holler and urge them on. But when their charges threaten to do one another serious mischief – we are, after all, the property of their masters and not to be damaged – they wade in, all fists themselves, and kick the little combatants to their feet, or haul them up by their hair or the scruff of the neck, holding them like polecats at arm's distance, wary of teeth, then pitch them back into the mob.

'And I am one of these snivelling barefoot brats. Six years old and indistinguishable, I hope – my survival depends on it – from the offspring of the lowest scullion. I have just enough sense of the danger I am in to make myself small so as not to attract attention. Some of those I am hiding among are palace slaves. Any one of them might point a finger and name me. Others again, just yesterday, were my playmates, little lords of all the world as I was. We avoid one another now. Turn our eyes away. Put the surging crowd between us.

'Imagine! To be at one moment the little pampered darling of your father's court, never more than twenty paces from your nurse or some watchful steward, the pet of your mother's maidservants – big girls with golden half-moons or butterflies in their ears that I liked to snatch at and jingle – and of slaves who had to approach me on their knees, even when all they were doing was offering a pile of shelled walnuts on a silver salver or a bowl to receive my tinkling piss. With a skin that had never known the touch of any but the finest cotton or silk, and in winter a lambswool undershirt. The possessor of a sleek bay pony, and a pet rabbit, and a wicker cage the size of my fist with a cricket in it to drum and chirp beside my pillow. To be at one moment Podarces, son of Laomedon, King of Troy, and in the next just one of a rabble of slave children, with a smell on me that I had taken till then to be the smell of another order of beings. A foul slave-smell that I clung to now in the hope that it would cling to me, since it was the only thing that could save me from drowning like my brothers, up there in the citadel, in my own blood.'

He sits, shaking his head. All this is so shameful, has for so long been secret in him. When he speaks again it is in a voice she barely knows.

'Leading away from the town, and from the place below it where we stand waiting in the dust, is a road, narrow, white, winding off across the plain, dwindling away into smoky haze. It looks quiet. It is empty as yet. I stand looking at it. That road leads to slavery – that's what I tell myself. It's the road *he* will drag me down. Slung across his shoulders like a sheep.

'I look up now and I can still see it. It's the road my other self went down. To a life where you and I, my dear, have never met, have never found one another. To a life I have lived entirely without you. In the same body perhaps,' he holds up his arm, 'with the same loose skin, the same ache in the knee-joints and thumbs. But one that for sixty years has known only drudgery and daily humiliation and blows. And that life too, I have lived, if only in a ghostly way. As a foul-smelling mockery of this one, that at any moment can rise to my nostrils and pluck at my robe and whisper, So there you are, old man Podarces.

'There are things,' he says, almost under his breath, 'that once we have touched them, once they have touched us, we can never throw off, however much we scrub away at ourselves, however high the gods set us. In our nostrils the stench is still there, the old filth *sticks*. The smell of those others – which was my smell too, the smell of the slave's life I was being dragged away to – I can never rub off.

'Sometimes late at night when I am sliding towards sleep, and in broad daylight too if I have been standing too long at some official ceremony, and the voice of my herald, Idaeus, has become a far-off drone in my ears like the buzzing of flies drunk on blood, it will be all around me. Foul, close, so thick it's a wonder that others don't hold their noses and turn away. And I am back there in the very midst of it, looking down that white-dust road into another life. And it means nothing, that other story. In this one the miraculous turnabout has never happened. I am just one more slave-thing like the rest, one among many. I look at my blackened hands and feet, the rags I am dressed in, and know that I have no more weight in the world than the droppings of the lowest beggar or street-sweeper. All I was promised by the poets of my father's court when they named my ancestors and sang of their high dealings with the gods, all the gods themselves promised, has been struck out, cancelled, and the little lord of all the pleasures I had taken myself to be, Podarces, son of Laome-don, is as dead as if he had choked on a sop of wine-soaked poppy-cake, or one of those sweat-stained butchers had cut his throat up there along with the rest of his brothers, and he had sat down astonished on the palace floor and watched his rare blood spread out across the pavement and drain away into a sluice.

'I take comfort from the others. Some of them are whimpering, but for the most part they are resigned. They've taken resignation in with their mother's milk. Misery is all they know, it's what they were born to. I resign myself. I let my old name go, since to speak it or hear it spoken would be death. I let it go, and with it that odd, old-fashioned little fellow it was tied to, who has choked on his bit of wine-soaked poppy-cake and been reborn as No One, and is waiting now, along with the rest, to be dragged out of the crowd and claimed and heard no more of.

'And then it happens. A breath, not my own, betrays me. "Podarces," it whispers, and I see peering in at me the black eyes of my sister, Hesione. When I shake my head and shrink back she speaks again. Louder this time.

'"Podarces!"

'Is she mad? Doesn't she realise?

'Because *he* is at her side, hulking and dark. Bareheaded but still fully armed. His leather cuirass stained with sweat, his body pouring forth the stink of his terrible exertions. Heracles, our father's enemy. The others know him too, and draw back. I am left alone under his gaze.

'It will happen now, I tell myself. Doesn't she realise? I close my eyes, hold my breath.

'But the hero laughs. He is in a mood, it seems, to be amused.

'"*That* thing?" he says. His voice is full of scorn. "You choose *that*? In the gods' name, why?"

'"Because he is my brother."

'He frowns. Leans down till his shaggy head is level with my own. The huge paw comes down, an iron clamp on my skull, and I feel his hot breath in my face. Smell the rank meatiness of him. Glance up after a moment under the brute weight of his palm.

'He is no longer glaring. But his smile! How easy it would be for him. Just a little more pressure of the fingertips, a turn of the hairy wrist, and my neck would snap.

'I meet his eyes and see there a lightning flicker that is the urge to do it. Because he can.

'"This is your brother?" he says, in a wondering tone. The small pig-eyes disappear in the muscled cheeks. "You're sure? It's really him?"

'"Of course it is," she tells him. "Wouldn't I know my own brother? Of course it's you, isn't it, Podarces, my dear?"

'I open my mouth but no sound comes.

'"And you wouldn't try, would you," he says,

my skull still locked in his grip, "to trick me? With a substitute?"

'He leans closer. "Well," he says playfully, "my little substitute, aren't *you* the lucky one?"

'He relaxes his hold and stretches upright. He looks, in his huge bulk, rather foolish. He is trying to please her by making a game of all this. And why not? She, too, is just a child. She is to go – another prize of war – as a gift to his friend Telamon, and he has told her she may have, as a gift of her own, whatever she chooses, anything her bright eyes light upon – expecting her to choose some gaudy trinket, a bauble to hang at her wrist or an ivory footstool from Punt, a bronze mirror to catch her smile in. But she is Laomedon's daughter. She has led him down to the horde of filthy, tear-stained urchins and searched among them and chosen me.

'"Well," he says, his slow mind working, "I promised you your choice. If this is what you choose, take him, take the brat, and let him be whatever you say he is, your brother or some nameless substitute, what does it matter? But since he is to be my fine gift to you, and to show that I am a man of my word, let his name, from now on, be Priam, the price paid, the gift given to buy your brother back from the dead. So that each time he hears himself named, this is what he will recall. That till I allowed you to choose him out of this filthy rabble, he was a slave like any other, a nameless thing, with no other life before him but the dirt and sweat of the slave's life. And in the secrecy of his own heart, *that*, for all the high titles the gods may heap upon him, is the life he will go on living day after day till his last breath."

'He narrows his eyes, sets his great meaty paw on my skull again, but this time with a deceptive gentleness, as if he were conferring a blessing. "Priam, the price paid. The substitute and pretender. A great one of the earth. But only by default. Because it pleases your fancy, little princess, to choose him, and mine to allow it."

'It was all mockery, you see. Young as I was, I knew mockery when I heard it, sneering contempt. That sort of low, back-handed nobility was all a Heracles was capable of. After all, he was a pretender himself. Only half a god, and that too by allowance and default.

'But his allowance was enough. Little shadow that I was of a dead prince, I caught the second breath they offered me and was delivered, called back under a new name. The gods had relented. Set back on my father's throne, I inherited his lands, his allies, married you, my dear – but a happy ending? Oh, I know what the *story* says. But after all those hours of being just one among so many – the ones for whom no miraculous turn would come, who would go on waiting in the dust and heat, and be carried off at last to a lifetime of slavery – I did not feel I'd been delivered. I had experienced something I could not un-experience and would never forget. What it means for your breath to be in another's mouth, to be one of those who have no story that will ever be told. After playing with me a little, and showing me what it was in their power to do, the gods had relented. They would allow me, in their high-handed, half-interested way, to cough up my bit of wine-soaked poppy-cake. But I had gone too far, you see, on the downward path to get back. I had the smell on me, here in my head, but also – I can smell it now – in my armpits, on my hands . . . ,' and his fine nose wrinkles with distaste.

'Priam, please,' Hecuba puts her fingertips to his lips. 'These things are so ugly.'

'But they happen,' he insists. 'And not just to other people. What I have been telling you happened to *me*. I stood in the midst of these things.'

He sees her shudder.

She is bewildered. He has also frightened her. She resents having been brought so close to what she does not want to know or think about. That moment of standing beside him, even in imagination, in a crowd of dirty, wailing children – the spawn, as he himself put it, of pedlars, whores, scullery maids – he should not have asked it of her. Dragging her in where she too would have that stink in her nostrils.

Concealing the repugnance she feels, she once more gives him the whole of her attention, but with real fear now of this mood that is on him, and of the even darker places he may lead her into.

'So,' he resumes, but with an irony in his tone that she recognises (she has heard it many times before, but only now sees the force of it), 'I was restored. When I slipped back into my old place in the world it was in a ghostly way and under a new name. As a substitute. For that little prince Podarces of whom nothing more would be heard or known. Except that *I* know him, I lived the first six years of his life. And many times over, in the darkness of my thoughts, as *he* predicted, I have made my way down into the underworld and sought him out, that small frightened child. To ask if he mightn't have some message for me, since he suffered my first death.

'A king, as you know, has to act in full assurance of what the gods have called him to, his high place in the world. He acts in the realm – that too is his kingdom – of the seen. But in my case the gift was a doubtful one. It was given then taken back again, and only in a joking, left-handed way restored. In me the assurance, the inner assurance, was lacking. Well, that is *my* affair. I have never spoken of it till now, even to you, my dear – though I expect you have sometimes wondered – and I hope that to others at least I have given no sign that there might be this, this *lack* in me. I have always, to the public view, been just what I appear to be. That is the discipline of kings. But to achieve it I have had to be more rigid than others. A little too punctilious, I know, in all that is due to ceremony. A stickler, as they say. For form, for the rules.

'All that belongs to the outward view. But there

is also an inward view,' and he falls silent a moment, as if for this view there might be no words, as there is no visible form, and she must catch what she can of it from what she can feel out in his silence.

'Well, as I said, none of that concerns anyone but myself and I've tried never to let it show. It's of no account what I happen to be feeling at any moment in my actual person – whether I have the toothache, or a belly swollen from eating too many peaches, or am raging with anger or impatience or desire – so long as I sit still and fill a space towards which others may look in reverence. So long, I mean, as I create the proper illusion. Only *I* know what it costs to *be* such an object. To rattle about like a pea in the golden husk of my . . . dazzling eminence. Never for even a moment to wobble or look flustered, or let the impressive effect be shaken by so much as the twitching of an eyelid or – god forbid! – a yawn. Or, in these latter days of my old age, by the trembling of a hand. I've played my part, and tried to let nothing peep out of the real man inside so much empty shining. I did it out of defiance of the gods, as well as in fearful reverence for them. In defiance of the fact that their first choice, all those years ago, was against me, as perhaps they have chosen against me a second time in this business of the war, so that I have now to be ransomed a second time – to ransom myself, as well as my son. By going to Achilles, not in a ceremonial way, as my symbolic self, but stripped of all glittering distractions and disguises, as I *am*.'

He sits with his hands clasped between his knees, suddenly weary. Hecuba too is silent. At last she sets her hand very gently on his shoulder and says, 'For the moment we'll speak no more of this. You go to your bath now. In the meantime I'll send a servant to summon our sons and the wisest of your councillors. Explain your plan to them. Let us see what *they* have to say of it.'

An hour later, Priam's sons, his many daughters and their husbands, and all his councillors and advisors are gathered in the inner court of the palace. They are abuzz, puzzled by the novelty of this late-morning summons and the news that the king has an announcement to make.

Only nine of the royal princes are Hecuba's sons. The rest, among them one or two of Priam's favourites, are the sons of other princesses, or they are bastards, though all bear the title of prince.

Once there was a full fifty of them. Those that remain, save for Helenus, who is a dedicated priest, are what Priam, in his more critical mood, calls heroes of the table and the dance; plump and soft-bellied most of them, with the exquisite manners of the courtier and a courtier's eye for the failings of others, along with a very practical talent for dropping into their father's ear the innocent fact or fiction that will do their rivals harm. For they are divided, these princes, even with a common enemy at the gate, into factions, all very watchful of one another. Only part of this has to do with court politics. The rest arises from the rivalry of their wives. Eager now to see what sort of mood their father is in, they turn as usual to Hecuba.

She enters and immediately begins whispering to Helenus – a bad sign, this – then moves, as a diversion, from one to another of the wives.

Careful as always to give each one of them the same cool but unaffected attention.

The wives are afraid of her, and it amuses the princes, who know their mother and her ways, that women who at home can be demanding, even intractable, go to water when this small, straight-backed woman puts her disconcerting questions, giving no indication in her smile of what she might think of the reply.

Today, Helenus too is on the move, consulting briefly with Deiphobus, leading Panyamus aside, and looking back over his shoulder to see which of the others may be watching.

Meanwhile Priam stands isolated and very nearly forgotten, till Polydorus, who is still little more than a child, a high-coloured, athletic boy with coal-black tresses and eyebrows that meet in the middle, launches boldly forward and greets his father very warmly and unselfconsciously with a kiss, which Priam, when he has recovered, returns.

The others, one after another, follow, greeting their father and receiving his blessing, though they do not, like Polydorus, kiss him. At least outwardly respectful, they set themselves to listen.

But when they hear, with growing alarm, what

the old man has in mind, they are filled with a misgiving that swells, as the questions spread among them, to outright consternation. How has he got hold of such a notion? It contradicts everything they have ever known of this grave and cautious figure who is their father. Challenges all they have ever demanded of the man, father or not, who is their king.

A king whose stable is the envy of every prince in the known world does not ride in a wagon drawn by *mules*. A king does not, in his own person, negotiate and deal. He has a herald to do that for him, in a voice that is skilled and trumpet-like, professionally trained in the laying down of challenges and the making of proclamations.

They turn from one to the other, all astir and eager to protest, but no one among them is willing to brave their father's temper and be the first man to speak. It is Deiphobus, the most smooth-mannered and eloquent of them, who steps forward at last.

'My dear lord,' he begins, 'you know what my brother Hector meant to me. How close we were. How of all my brothers he was dearest to me, as I believe I was to him. There is no danger I would not face to bring him home to your house, my lord, and to my poor mother's arms.'

Yes, yes, Priam thinks, that is all very well, but what have you done more than the rest? Beat your breast, fouled your hair with earth, wept a little. You are young and hardy. Even an old man like me can do that much.

'Sir,' Deiphobus resumes, 'Father, this plan of yours is not only new and unheard of, it not only puts your precious life at risk, it also exposes to insult – and this, I know, you value every bit as much as life itself – your royal image. Do you really imagine that a man who has no respect for the body of his enemy, for the laws of honourable behaviour before men and the gods, who in the frenzy of his pride and wrath, his madness, daily violates the corpse of the noblest hero our world has known, that such a man would not take delight in hauling down your kingly image and dragging that too in the dust? And what then of all you hold in custody? The sacred spirit of our city, the lives of each one of us. I say nothing of the treasure you will be carrying. That is mere earth-stuff, metal, however finely worked. It is dispensible. You, my lord, are the treasure we cannot allow to be lost. You are what matters to us.

'Sir, you have for the whole of your life been a king. Ordinary desires and needs and feelings are not unknown to you – I know that, you are my father; but you have, you *can* have, in your kingly role, no part in them – they are not in your royal sphere. And are you now to wring Achilles' heart by appealing to those very feelings of the ordinary man that it has been the whole business of your life to remain aloof from?

'I beg you, sir, be patient like the rest of us. Can you really believe that Hector, who was so proud, who loved you and cared so much for your royal dignity, and fought and poured his life out to preserve it, would thank his father for clasping the knees of his killer in a merely *human* way, and laying all the glory of Troy in the dust? He would weep, my lord, as I do –' and at this Deiphobus, unable to go on, dashes the tears from his eyes and turns away.

Priam lowers his head. When he raises it again his look is grave but his eyes, for all the power of emotion in him, are dry.

'Deiphobus, you speak to me as a son, and I am

sorry if what I have it in my head to do offends or shames you. I have had a good sixty years now to consider the splendour and limitations of what it is to be a king. You speak, too, as a brother. I know how much you loved Hector, and how deeply affected you have been by the loss of a man we all cherished and depended on. You ask me to stand, as I have always done, at a kingly distance from the human, which in my kingly role, as you say, I can have no part in. But I am also a father. Mightn't it be time for me to expose myself at last to what is merely human? To learn a little of what that might be, and what it is to bear it as others do? I know I am an old man, feeble in body and ill-equipped to go venturing out at this late date into a world of change and accident. But as you know, I am also stubborn, and I have not survived this long without a certain degree of toughness. Perhaps this –' and he glances quickly in Hecuba's direction – 'is the time to show it.'

Cassandra is there, pale and distracted-looking, only half-attentive. Her brothers turn to her now in the hope that their father, who is fond of the poor deluded creature, will listen to her.

But Cassandra has nothing to say. Her god has

withdrawn. He no longer visits and inflames her. Numb with grief for her brother Hector, she feels only a dulled indifference to what is happening around her; even to what is happening, or about to happen, to herself. As if it had already occurred, and too long ago now to be of any consequence. When her brothers look towards her – those brothers who once mocked her searing visions – she shakes her head and remains dumb.

At last, since no one else seems willing to speak, Polydamas comes forward. Not one of Priam's sons, or even a son-in-law, but one of the wisest of the Trojans.

'My lord Priam,' he begins, 'you know the reverence and great affection in which I hold you. Firstly, on my friend Hector's account, because I thought of him always as a brother and of you, therefore, as a second father. Even more, because for the whole of my life what I have chiefly cared for is order, and for as long as I have had experience of the world, you have been the great upholder of order among us; none more pious, none more punctilious in what is owed to the gods, but also to us, your subjects, who look to you as the fountainhead of all that keeps Troy civil and just. But that, my lord, is the limit of what we have a right to ask, and all that the gods too can demand. They made you a king. A proper kingliness of spirit and presence is all that they, or we, can require of you, my lord, and all, in these sad times, that you need properly ask of yourself.

'I beg you, spare yourself this ordeal. Do not, for the affection we all bear you, expose yourself to the hazards of war and of the road, or to the indignities that Achilles and any other Greek who happens along might heap upon you. Be kind to your old age. Relieve yourself of this unnecessary task.'

Priam considers the man. He is pleased with what Polydamas has said. Pleased too that it offers him something to say in return that will make clearer his reasons for what he has determined on.

'Thank you, Polydamas. You are too generous in your tribute, but I am grateful. What you have to say of order and kingliness does you credit. If I reject your advice, it is not because I do not value it. I do. And I value *you,* not least because you were my son's dear friend and I know he loved and listened to you.

'It is true that the gods made me a king, but they

also made me a man, and mortal. Gave me life and all that comes with it. All that is sweet. All that is terrible too, since only what we know we must lose is truly sweet to us. The gods themselves know nothing of this, and in this respect, perhaps, may envy us. But not in the end. Because, in the end, what we come to is what time, with every heart-beat and in every moment of our lives, has been slowly working towards: the death we have been carrying in us from the very beginning, from our first breath. Only we humans can know, endowed as we are with mortality, but also with conscious-ness, what it is to be aware each day of the fading in us of freshness and youth; the falling away, as the muscles grow slack in our arms, the thigh grows hollow and the sight dims, of whatever manly vigour we were once endowed with. Well, all that *happens*. It is what it means to be a man and mortal, and as men we accept it. Less easy to accept is what follows from it.

'One day war comes, and what the moment demands is strength of nerve and sinew, quickness of eye and foot and hand. An old man has no part to play then but that of a bystander or passive looker-on. And if all goes badly, if the citadel falls and the killers come pouring through the streets – men whose blood is a roaring lion in them, who go raging from house to house looking for women and children to destroy, and feeble old men, old bystanders and lookers-on, to run down and slaughter – it will mean nothing then, nothing at all, if one of those feeble old men happens also to be a king. When the dogs claw at one another's backs in their frenzy to get at his entrails, when they gnaw at the skull and the misshapen feet, and tear without shame at the old man's private parts, the source of so many noble sons and daughters.

'One of the chief concerns of a good king is the image he presents, and most of all, as he grows older, the image that other men will keep of him when he is gone. That is what I am concerned with now, in these last days of my kingship.

'I cannot stop what may be about to occur. That I leave, as I must, to the gods. If the last thing that happens to me is to be hunted down in the heart of my citadel, and dragged out by the feet, and shamelessly stripped and humiliated, so be it. But I do not want that to be the one sad image of me that endures in the minds of men. The image I mean to leave is a living one. Of something so new and unheard of that when men speak my name it will stand forever as proof of what I was. An act, in these terrible days, that even an old man can perform, that only an old man *dare* perform, of whom nothing now can be expected of noise and youthful swagger. Who can go humbly, as a father and as a man, to his son's killer, and ask in the gods' name, and in their sight, to be given back the body of his dead son. Lest the honour of all men be trampled in the dust.'

Priam's voice breaks and he turns aside to hide his tears. Hecuba's hand is there to steady him. The rest too are moved. And they see, as Hecuba does, that there is no point in further argument. Foolish as the old man's plan may be, they can only reconcile themselves and let him have his way.

It is early afternoon now. Priam, already attired in the plain white robe of his vision, with Hecuba beside him and his head nodding a little, is seated under an awning in the open courtyard. He is waiting while Hippothous and Dius, two of the royal princes, supervise the getting ready of a cart. Helenus has been dispatched to assemble the precious objects he will take from his treasury, the cauldrons, tripods, armour and the rest that will make up Hector's ransom.

At last, with a buzz of approval from the crowd, Hippothous and Dius reappear and a four-wheeled cart is trundled in, a fine new one, the marks of the adze still visible on its timbers. The twelve-spoked wheels are elaborately carved and painted, a wickerwork canopy covers the tray. All is of the most ingenious design and intricate workmanship.

Behind, attended by two grooms, walks the king's herald, Idaeus, plainly but splendidly attired, bearing the royal staff; and with him, in an impressive cavalcade, Priam's ceremonial chariot with two thoroughbred horses between the shafts, elegant, high-stepping creatures all liquid muscle and nerve, their manes plaited with thread-of-gold.

Priam is immediately in a rage. He leaps from his seat, and the princes, who know what he is when he is roused, draw back.

'Are you deaf?' he shouts. 'Did not one of you hear me when I spoke? Or am I so old and feeble now that you no longer feel obliged to take the least notice of what I say? I asked for a cart, an ordinary mule cart, not this . . . carnival wagon! You have done this because you are still thinking in the old way. I told you, I *tried* to tell you, that my vision was of something new. Now, this time listen. Go down to the marketplace and find me a common work cart, such as a man might carry logs in, or fired bricks or a load of hay. The mules should be strong, the driver too, but nothing more is required. No chariot, no horses. I will ride in the cart on the crossbench beside the driver. Now, this time bring what I've asked for. I won't ask again!'

So it is that there appears in the palace court-yard, not long after, a stocky fellow of fifty or so, bull-shouldered, shock-headed, with a country-man's spade-shaped beard, rough-cut and of an iron-grey colour; a carter with a reputation among the market people for being reliable enough but, when he has had a drink or two, a bit of a madcap, and the owner of two strong black mules. His name is Somax.

The princes, who found the man waiting in the marketplace to be hired, have assured him he has committed no wrong, it is not for that reason they are bringing him in; but he is apprehensive just the same when they lead him, in his homespun robe and broken sandals, into the palace yard where so many royal persons are assembled.

A plain workman, he has had no experience till now of princes. He is dazzled by the cleanness, the whiteness of everything here. The arms, necks, faces of the women, of some of the men too, who look as if they have never seen sunlight. The columns, the walls of polished stone, the pavement with not a straw in sight. The plump-breasted fan-tailed doves that go strutting around a fountain in a formal way, as if they had been trained to do it, dipping their beaks into its pool.

He is surprised, too, by the tallness of these Trojans. And their voices, which are thin and high-pitched, unlike his own and those of the folk he lives among.

He hangs his head and studies the pavement between his feet. He is here, he knows, not for himself but because of his mules, and especially the smaller of the two, which, the moment they entered the marketplace, caught the eye of one of the princes as she does everyone's – she is such a plain charmer.

A little black thing, strong in the withers but also dainty, her winning nature has much to do with her intelligence, which is there for all to see, and with the fact that she notices people and responds in such a lively way to their interest. Beauty, he calls her. He has raised her up himself, coaxing and sweet-talking her, rewarding her with tidbits from his palm, scratching her downy ears and whispering his small secrets to her.

In the tavern where he goes to enjoy a little company, to hear a joke or two and to escape in lightheadedness the harshness of his life, he talks so warmly and so often of his little mule that he is teased for it with all sorts of coarse but joking suggestions; and it is true, he is a little in love with the creature.

So it is the mule that has brought him here, and because of her that he now stands in the royal palace, in a courtyard crowded with princes and their ladies, and rather fearful, under their gaze, of what might be expected of him. He does not recognise at first the spare old fellow, very plainly dressed in a white robe, who gets up out of a chair, comes close, and subjects him to scrutiny. He has seen King Priam only at a distance, an imposing figure, long-boned and tall, standing very straight and stiff in his chariot – never face to face like this. He is surprised how old he looks. How sunken and deeply scored the cheeks, and deeply set in their sockets and milky pale the eyes under their straggle of white brows.

'So,' Priam says at last. 'They have explained to you what we are to do?'

The man nods. He does not know how he should address the king and is conscious, among so much lilting and lisping, of his own harsh-sounding gutturals.

He glances for help to the two princes, who frown but nod. 'They have,' he ventures. 'I am to drive to the Greek camp.'

The king draws closer. The carter thinks he might be taking a whiff of him. He shifts uncomfortably and lifts his shoulders in the looseness of his robe. His nose itches and he has a powerful urge to rub it, but resists. All this, he thinks, along with his smell, the old man, who has come very close now, is taking into account and judging. At last, with no change of expression, the king turns to face the princes.

'I like the look of this fellow,' he announces in a

good clear voice, and all the members of the court take a second look at him and clap their hands – but in a restrained and formal way, with a sound so pit-a-pat small that the pigeons are barely disturbed in their dipping and promenading.

The man Somax is inclined to chuckle, but he restrains himself. Likes the look of me, does he? Well there's something! He thinks of what his cronies at the tavern will have to say of this. At the same moment one of the princes makes a gesture, and with a grinding and creaking that is quite out of place among so many subdued voices and the gurgling and cooing of the pigeons, his cart is wheeled in. The mules prick their ears at the sight of him, and he immediately feels more securely himself, more solidly at home in his body and lighter in spirit for their presence.

Priam meanwhile has been regarding this rough-looking fellow who is to be the sole companion of his journey and is confirmed once again in the rightness of his project. The carter resembles so completely the figure in his dream.

For the whole half-century of his kingship, the herald who has attended Priam on all ceremonial occasions, to carry the royal staff, and raise his voice and speak for him when speech is required, has borne the old Dardanian name of Idaeus, though whether the man who appeared at his side was at every point the same Idaeus he has never found the need to ask. It is the office and the name that matters, not the person, and it is in the light of this identification of name with office, and the continuity of the office in the name, that Priam, who has already made one bold decision, is led now to another.

He turns to the carter, and in a voice that is meant to be intimate rather than peremptory, but loud enough for the whole company to hear, announces: 'One other thing. I am accustomed, on all occasions when I leave my palace, to have a herald with me. He is called Idaeus. Since you will be my only companion on this journey, that is how I will think of you, and how you, my man, should think of yourself. From now on your name is Idaeus.'

The carter glances about him, believing there must be something here that he has failed to grasp. He shuffles, rubs his nose rather vigorously with the heel of his hand, looks up under wrinkled brows in the hope that he may catch some clue from the reaction of the crowd.

There is a stirring among the princes of subdued unease. Once again this readiness on their father's part to change on a whim what has been for so long fixed and accepted dismays them.

As for the carter, who is quite out of his depth now and wonders what further madness these high folk will demand of him – what can he do but drop his head and mutter, very low and without much enthusiasm, 'Very well, sir. Right, my lord.'

But in fact it is not 'very well' with him, not at all. His name is Somax. It fits him, he has always thought, rather well. He has been comfortable with it, warm and very much himself, for a good fifty years, give or take a little. It guarantees the breath that passes in and out of his mouth; is an assurance, after a good night's sleep, that the spirit that has left his body and gone wandering off to all sorts of places will find its way back to the particular pile of straw where he is lying, and be recognised and taken in. It is the name under which he married his dear one and became the father of five children – none of them, alas, now living – and under which he has always conducted himself, so far as a poor man can, honestly, and kept himself in good odour with the gods. Will they recognise him, he wonders, under this new one?

Idaeus indeed! Mightn't they take it amiss, those high ones, that after fifty years under one denomination he should suddenly present himself under another? Mightn't they see as a kind of presumption this juggling with the high dignity of heralds and such, this taking on of 'Idaeus' by such a plain low-born fellow?

He shuffles. Feels a crawling under his robe as if all his lice had been stirred up and were on the move. Something about the life he has lived all these years, the hardships, the losses he has suffered, and the way he has forced himself to go on and endure, is being set aside and made light of. That is what he feels.

So when the royal princes, in their affected tones and with a deference so out of proportion to his real status that it can only, he thinks, be a form of subtle mockery, with an 'Idaeus this', and a 'my *dear* Idaeus that', begin to make requests and give orders, he feels increasingly uneasy, then silently, sullenly affronted.

Perhaps he is wrong and no offence is intended; they are simply acting in accordance with their father's odd wishes, and however foolish and effeminate they may appear, this is the way they always speak. But he smoulders just the same, and in spirit at least clenches his fist. He steadies himself by turning to his mules, who stand patient amid so much fluster, waiting for him, in the usual way, to give some indication of when they should move. Beauty the one is called, and the other Shock, though there is no reason why anyone here should know this, and he decides, in a spirit of quiet resistance, to keep these names to himself.

Meanwhile piles of treasure are being brought in: copper cauldrons and tripods, ewers, urns, cups, ceremonial arms and armour; some of it – the cauldrons for instance – so weighty that it takes two servants to heave the pieces up onto the tray. Slowly, the wagon, which has known nothing till now, as the driver could tell them, but winter wood, or hides or stacks of forage, is tight-packed with precious objects.

To the watchers, as the treasure is assembled piece by piece, it is as if what is taking shape there, in all its shining parts, is a body – that of their dear kinsman Hector, for which in their hearts, filled now with the hope that comes from wishing, the hoard has already been exchanged.

At last, when all is done, Hecuba sends her steward for a jar of clear springwater and a cup of wine for a drink offering.

She herself takes the ewer from her steward's hand, and when Priam has turned back the sleeves of his pure white robe, sprinkled his fingers and dried them with a cloth, she hands him the cup and he prays aloud. Raising his face to where the gods, in their high court, will be looking on, he allows a few drops of the mellow wine to spill on the pavement and prays again.

The carter, peering up from under his brows, is impressed by the solemnity of the occasion, but the moment lasts too long. His nose begins to itch.

At last the tension breaks and someone notices, high up under thin clouds, a bird hanging with wings extended in the blue.

Mmm, the carter thinks, a chickenhawk. Riding the updraught and hanging there, on the lookout for a fieldmouse in the furrows below, or a venturesome hamster or vole.

But prompted by his mother, the priest Helenus proclaims it an eagle. The carter is surprised at this, though no one else appears to be. The whole assembly raises its eyes, and the murmur that fills the court is one of wonder and relief.

Clear for all to see, Jove's emblem and messenger is hovering there, holding them, these mighty representatives of Troy, and the many thousands of people outside the palace, in the city and in the villages and provinces beyond, in the quivering net of its celestial attention and concern.

Each day at first light the people of Troy crowd the ramparts of the city, the colonnade before the Scaean gate and the broad streets leading to the central square, to watch the Trojan army with shields newly polished, and breastplates and helmets flashing, march out to the field. The passing of this or that hero among them occasions cheers. Some of the little girls in the crowd have gathered flowers and rush forward to pelt their favourites. There is laughter as vivid red petals spatter a warrior's breast. The air is just heating, and the men sweat inside their leather, but step out briskly in close order. The day is new and still to be won.

Then, in the shadows of late afternoon, in the same numbers but more quietly now, until the stillness is broken by the shrieks of some wife or mother, the crowd assembles for a second time to see their defenders, all streaked with sweat and dust, or in bandages and bleeding, troop home. Some – too many – lie on pallets borne by their squires or comrades, groaning or already stiff in death. Others, propped up on one elbow, call to their family or to friends and neighbours in the crowd – 'See, I am alive, I'm still living.' Or with teeth clenched in silent pain, they clasp the hand of a wife or child who walks, half-laughing, half-weeping, at their side. All this till eleven days ago when Hector was slain and all fighting between the two sides was suspended.

Now, at three in the afternoon, news spreads from yard to yard and stall to stall in the swarming market that a procession is gathering at the palace gate.

Labourers in neat-skin aprons with a hammer at their belt call down from the scaffolding of the buildings they are at work on and point, for though the city stands, and has stood for nearly ten years now on the brink of destruction, new houses are still being built and old ones repaired or added to. In spite of alarms, and many deprivations and shortages, the life of the city goes on. Linen is still spread to dry on quince trees or rosemary bushes. Hives have to be visited each day and honey gathered from dripping racks. Cats have still to be set to keep mice out of granaries and the cellars where oil jars are kept, pine logs trimmed and stacked in piles against the winter, trenches dug and cisterns maintained so that the autumn rain when it comes pelting will not run off down the sides of the bluff along which the city is spread. Magistrates, sweating in the late-afternoon heat, have still to hear witnesses and endure the long-winded addresses of rival advocates in a case of assault or murder, since even under threat from a common enemy citizens still harbour grudges and pursue with undiminished bitterness long-standing quarrels or vendettas, and wars still break out among neighbours over the most trivial affronts.

But today, all this busy activity comes to a halt. Crowds race through the streets and push for a place on the city walls. Boys leave off their arm-wrestling, or their games of jackstones or tag, and scramble out between the legs of their elders to be in the front row of spectators; among greybeards, pickpockets, idlers and loungers of every sort, women with a child on their hip and another in hand that they drag along howling, sellers of perfume, sellers of pickles, sellers of fried grasshoppers and of almonds still soft in their velvety green shells, prosperous shopkeepers and their wives who have set a reluctant assistant to watch over their wares while they bustle, fat and breathless, to the nearest vantage point.

Just on three, a cart drawn by two black mules and driven by a man the whole town recognises as a simple carter, Somax, the son of Astrogon, lumbers slowly out of the palace gates and downhill towards the square.

On the crossbench beside the driver, very stiff-looking in a plain white robe, sits the king, Priam, severely upright and with no fillet on his brow, no staff in his hand, no amulet or armband.

On either side of the cart, and in rows behind, sauntering along in a casual way and, when the cart slows or comes to a halt, stumbling a little as they crowd in one against the next, come the king's remaining sons: Helenus, Paris – the crowd names them as they pass – Agathon, Deiphobus and Antiphonus, Dius, Pammon, Hippothous, and the youngest of all the royal princes, the boy Polydorus.

The mules pull and sweat; the cart is heavy. Some heaped-up load covered by a cloth is in the tray. The driver is anxious. He makes more fuss than seems strictly necessary about negotiating the cartwheels over the big cobbles. Priam, like the statue of himself at the entrance to the temple, sits stiff and square, his gaze fixed rigidly ahead.

It is such an unaccustomed sight, so sober, so stripped of all finery and show, that the crowd, for all its high spirits, does not know how to react. No one thinks it appropriate to cheer. Is the city's wealth being taken to safety somewhere deep in the country? Is the king deserting them?

They watch the cart stop before the high wooden gate, see the bar raised, hear the great locks snap.

From the walls the crowd, buzzing now with excited speculation, watches the procession wind downhill to the stone trough among riven pines where in the old days, before the war, the Trojan women used to go to steep their washing in the spring. Then on to the lookout with its lone, windswept fig.

Here the little group breaks up.

The cart lurches on and, with Jove's eagle sitting high above, takes the high road that leads out across the plain. The royal princes, singly or in groups, turn back and make their way, bend after dog-legged bend, uphill.

Whatever it was is over. Or, mysteriously, has just begun.

Just on dusk, with the light begining to fade but the air still heated and thick, the wagon creaked down to where Scamander, in its leisurely winding across the plain, scoops two channels out of the bone-white gravel of its bed. One bubbles and is milky-green. The other, which runs deeper, is a smooth-flowing blue. Both were shallow enough at this time of the year to be forded. Glossy-leafed rosebay bushes grew in flowering clumps on the islands between, and in the air above, swifts, with an excited crying, wheeled in high wide circles feeding on midges or skimmed the surface of the stream.

'Well, my lord,' the driver announced, 'we've come this far safe enough.'

Rather stiff in the joints, he eased himself down from the cart and, whispering a word or two in the ear of the little off-side mule, secured the reins to the trunk of a tamarisk; then stood waiting with his hand extended for Priam to get down.

But the king, his chin raised so that the loose skin at his throat trembled with the effort, continued to sit.

Dear me, the driver thought, he'll get an awful pain in his back if he goes on sitting like that. He scratched his head, uncertain how he should address the king or what he might say to tempt him down. He cleared his throat, and the king, reminded of his presence, spoke.

'Thank you,' he said quietly. 'I shall just stay here in the wagon with the body of my son.'

The driver blinked.

Ah, he thought, so that's it. The old king's thoughts, leaping ahead, past all the many difficulties they were yet to pass, had already arrived at the end of their business. It was the body of Prince Hector, freshly washed and shrouded in white linen, that he saw glowing out of the bed of the cart. Well, that was foolish of course, but entirely understandable.

Very tactfully, his heart softened by fellow-feeling, since he too was a father, he allowed himself the deception of pretending he had mis-heard. 'Oh,' he said. 'If it's the treasure you're afraid for, my lord, that'll be safe enough. Beauty here will keep an eye on it, won't you, my love?'

The little mule pricked her ears at the sound of her name and turned her head.

The driver chuckled. 'See, my lord, how she knows every word I speak to her? She's as good as any watchdog, I promise. She won't let them get away with even a copper coin, will you, my pet?'

The old king saw his error then. A flush came to his cheek. Looking very slight and frail, he moved to get down, and the driver, relieved of a difficulty he had thought he might not be able to resolve, reached up to take Priam's hand. He had acted on impulse. Only when he saw how startled Priam was at this unaccustomed touch did it occur to him that he might have committed some affront to the king's sacred person.

But Priam had already recovered. Far from taking offence, he seemed grateful – or so the man thought – for the ready consideration of his need. With great courtesy he thanked the driver, and with one or two twinges, but no lack of royal dignity, allowed himself to be handed down.

'That's it, my lord,' the carter told him, 'you'll see. We'll have a nice rest here, and maybe even a bite to eat.' He thought he should sow that seed early, since he had had nothing himself since close on dawn. 'We've got shade from the heat and plenty of cover. No one will spy us here.'

He led the king down through soft sand to the water's edge.

'It's an easy enough crossing at this time of the year, though it can be wicked at others.'

Twisting the homespun of his robe in his fist and hoiking it manfully up to his knees, he took a step, sandals and all, into the stream.

The bottom was sandy, the shallows so still and clear you could see the fingerlings that, alert to this sudden large intrusion into their world, formed a silvery arrowhead of light under the surface and came darting in to investigate. All quiver and nerve, they nosed in and nudged and nibbled at him.

The carter, hands on knees, leaned over to study them.

'Hello, little ones,' he called.

But they had already decided that he was an object of no interest. In a single shivering movement, they wheeled and cut away.

With a laugh the carter followed the flash they made under the surface, then straightened and turned back to where Priam, looking uncertain and out of place, stood watching. He's like a child, he thought, a bit on the slow side. Or a man who's gone wandering in his sleep and doesn't know where he is or how he got there.

Well, it was clear no orders were to be expected from that direction. If they were to move forward it was up to him. But how should he begin? How, he wondered, would that other, the *real* Idaeus, have acted? He had never in all his life till now had to do with any but simple folk like himself, eaters of sheep's cheese and raw garlic, women laying out a bit of washing to dry on a bush beside the road, half-naked children, their heads shaven against lice, who came to a wicker fence to wave as he passed, calling, 'Hey grandad, where are you off to? Ride us, why don't you, to the big wall.' He would have to rely on native wit, and such bits of experience as are common to all, whether the gods in their wisdom have set us high or low.

'You'd feel better, sir,' he ventured, 'if you were to do as I have, and come down and dabble your feet a little. The coolness of the water will buck you up no end. There's a good hour till sundown, and we'll go safer on the other side if we wait till dark.'

The king looked startled, as if this voice had come from nowhere. But the driver, bolder now, thought that having once begun he had better go right on. He climbed back up the shelving bank, knelt, and since the king offered no resistance, but simply stood looking down at what he was doing as if it were happening with no agency at all, unlaced first one, then the other of his sandals, each time with an upward glance of apology for anything there might be in the action, or in his touch, that was unseemly.

Like an obedient toddler, Priam lifted one foot then the other till the sandals were off and sitting side by side on the lip of sand; then, with a glance towards the driver, who nodded to urge him on, took three uncertain steps into the stream. When, as the driver had promised, he felt the cooling effect, he smiled, looked back to where the driver was still crouched on the bank above, and nodded. Then stood staring down at his naked feet, which were very bony and white, as the same little slivers of light came flashing in, and nudged and tickled. He observed with amusement that they found the royal feet every bit as disappointing and without interest as the driver's.

He was a rough fellow, this companion he had chosen, with no notion, so far as he could see, of what was proper, but he did know his way about, and there was so much simple modesty and good-will in the man, and so much tact in the way he made his suggestions, that Priam found nothing objectionable in him. It was not reverence he lacked, only a knowledge of the forms. And out here, perhaps, and in the world the fellow moved in, such forms might not be altogether useful.

He indicated to the man that he should sit, then sat very contentedly himself, letting the goodness of the cool clean water extend its reviving benefit from his feet to his whole being.

His spirits, which till now had been clouded by uncertainty and a fear of so much that was still unknown, cleared and lightened.

Meanwhile the driver had released a leather satchel from his shoulder and was laying out its contents on a square of clean if ragged cloth.

'It might be as well,' he suggested, 'if you took a bite to eat, my lord. We won't get another opportunity, and we've got a goodish journey before us. Just a mouthful. To keep your strength up.'

Priam shook his head.

The carter nodded. He looked at the good things he had taken from the bag.

There were olives, plump black ones. Pumpkin seeds. A stack of little griddlecakes of a kind Priam had never seen before, of a golden yellow colour and about the size of a medallion. The man, his Idaeus, looked at them, he thought, rather regretfully. No doubt the fellow was hungry.

With great courtesy the king said, 'Please, do eat something yourself. The little cakes look good and I have no objection.'

'Well, it's true, sir, I've taken nothing since early morning and it's already after five.' He took up one of the cakes.

'These little cakes, now, since they've caught your eye, sir – pikelets they are, or griddlecakes as some people call them – were made by my daughter-in-law. Best buckwheat flour, good thick buttermilk, just a drop of oil. The buttermilk has to be of a cream colour, and thick, so that when you pour it out of the crock it comes in a slow stream. Then the batter is ladled onto a skillet over hot stones. My son, the gods rest him, set the stones up in a new way, out of affection, you know, for my daughter-in-law, to make things easier for her, and so that the cakes would cook faster and be the sweeter for it. He was a clever fellow in that way, always thinking about things. And it has an effect, it really does. It's a real pleasure to watch the batter bubbling and setting and turning a golden brown, as you can see, around the edges. The lightness comes from the way the cook flips them over. Very neat and quick you have to be. The daughter-in-law, she's a good girl, uses her fingers – it's a trick you have to learn – and if she happens to burn them she pops her fingers into her mouth quick smart like this –' and by way of illustration, he popped one of the little cakes into his mouth, almost unnoticed it might have been under the influence of his talk.

'Ummm, you can taste the lightness! I've eaten twenty of these little fellows at a single sitting. Not out of greed, sir, but for the joy they bring to the heart. The flavour comes from the buttermilk, but owes something as well, I dare say, to the good humour of the cook, and the skill, you know, of her fingers in the flipping. That too you can taste. But maybe for that you have to have been there to see her do it. So quick and light,' and with thumb and finger not quite touching, he turned his hairy wrist in the air to give Priam some notion of it, but also to revive his own happy memory. 'Are you quite sure, my lord, that you won't take just a bite of one?'

When Priam shook his head the man said, 'Well at least, sir, take a few drops of wine. To wet your mouth a little and bless the occasion.'

Priam, who realised now that the man mentioned it that he was rather dry, but also because the fellow was so pleasant and persuasive, agreed to this, and Idaeus, with a happy smile, passed him the flask.

'There now,' he said, as Priam took a modest swig, 'that'll do you no end of good.'

And it was true, it did. Priam took another, more copious mouthful.

'You see, sir, a fellow like me, who needs his strength for hard work, has to know a little about what is good for the body as well as the spirit. Now – if you'll allow the suggestion, my lord – not to be light-headed after the wine, you really should take a bite of something. It won't help our business if halfway along we get sick with faintness. A man needs to be practical about these things, to help the spirit along, if you'll entertain the thought, sir, with a good comfortable feeling in the belly and the legs. There's no harm in that. If the one is to be considered, so must the other. We're children of nature, my lord. Of the earth, as well as of the gods.'

So it was that Priam, who did feel himself a little faint, but not without a fear that in this he might be compromising the purity of his mission, allowed himself to be persuaded and took one of the little cakes in his fingers, broke off a morsel, and tasted.

It was very good. What the driver had said of its lightness was true, and of its effect on the spirit. He finished the cake but declined a second. Abstemiousness was native in him. He based a certain sense of his formal relationship to nature on his being not too dependent upon it; despite what the driver had said, and very pertinently too, of their being doubly tied both to the gods and to the earth.

When he set out on this business he had understood quite clearly that he would be exposing

himself to things he had not previously encountered. That was the price of the new. But as he sat
now with the golden taste of the pancake in his
mouth and another drop of wine on his lips, he
saw that what was new could also be pleasurable.

This sitting with your feet in cooling water, for
instance, that ran over them and away.

The little fish that came to investigate, and said,
No, nothing to be got out of this one.

The wheeling and piping of swifts, which grew
both in volume and excitement as the day's light
thickened.

Of course these things were not new in themselves. The water, the fish, the flocks of snub-tailed
swifts had always been here, engaged in their own
lives and the small activities that were proper to
them, pursuing their own busy ends. But till now
he had had no occasion to take notice of them.
They were not in the royal sphere. Being unnecessary to royal observance or feeling, they were in the
background, and his attention was fixed always on
what was central. Himself. The official activity
that was his part in any event or scene, the formal
pose it was his duty to maintain and make shine.

When he went out on a boar hunt, for example,

he was surrounded by attendants young and old, some on foot, others on horseback, each with a particular role to perform in the ceremonial play; as beaters and dog-handlers, as court officials in charge of the provisions, as tenders of the wagons that would carry them, as squires and cup-bearers who would set up the tables in the woods where at midday the whole company would eat, or as the one, specially chosen for the occasion, whose honour it would be, when the boar had been har-ried and brought to bay, and lowered its head and stood stamping and foaming among the leaves, to pass him the lance he was to cast – often, given the feebleness of his arm these days, in a merely formal way – before some other, younger man stepped in and made the kill.

He was symbolically at the centre, as form and his own royal dignity demanded, but could have no part in the merely physical business, all panic and sweat, of rushing through the brush to where half a ton of steaming flesh and bone waited to be hacked, and thrust at, and brought crashing to earth.

The boar was his, of course, and at the end of the day was presented to him – or rather, he was presented to it – and a little of the beast's thick blood smeared on his brow. Men cheered, applauding his prowess. All this quite formal, and not to be taken literally. He would pour a libation, and with the gods' assent some of the boar's fierce energy, and hot muscle and hotter breath, would fatten his spirit. It was a mystery. Part of a world of ceremony, of high play, that was eternal and had nothing to do with the actual and immediate, with *this* particular occasion, or *this* boar, or *this* king. Even the landscape it took place in was freed of its particular elements – the kind and colour of the leaves, or whether the day was sunlit or mistily overcast, the earth dry or muddy underfoot. The realm of the royal was representational, ideal. Everything that was merely accidental – a broken thong, the cry of pain from a beater where the boar's tusk found bone and real blood drenched the leaves – all this was to be ignored, left to fall away into the confused and confusing realm of the incidental and ordinary.

His whole life was like that, or had been. But out here, he discovered, everything was just itself. That was what seemed new.

In being just itself, neither more nor less, each

thing appeared to him in a form he barely recognised; self-absorbed, separate, too busy with its own life of running from here to there like the water, or seeking out food like the fishlings and the noisy circle of swifts, to take much account of one old man who had wandered in among them to settle for a time and then pass on.

It was bewildering, all that, but not unpleasurable. On the whole he felt easy with himself, both in body and spirit; comfortably restored. (He waved off a cloud of midges that seemed especially attracted by his royal sweat.) But would any of it have been possible, he wondered, if he had been accompanied in the usual way by his other Idaeus? Of course, he would have been treated with the greatest consideration, but there would have been none of the surprises this new Idaeus offered.

He worked his toes in the coolness and found himself chuckling. Most surprising of all was the way the fellow let his tongue run on, with no fear at all, it seemed, of being taken for a mere rattle or chatterer.

What he had to say, if you regarded it strictly, was unnecessary. It had no point or use. The wonder, given this, was that it did so little harm – none at all in fact – to the fellow's dignity. There was something here, Priam thought, that he needed to think about.

In his own world a man spoke only to give shape to a decision he had come to, or to lay out an argument for or against. To offer thanks to one who had done well, or a reproof, either in anger or gentle regret, to one who had not. To pay a compliment whose decorative phrases, and appeals to vanity or family pride, were fixed and of ancient and approved form. Silence, not speech, was what was expressive. Power lay in containment. In keeping hidden, and therefore mysterious, one's true intent. A child might prattle, till it learned better. Or women in the seclusion of their own apartments.

But out here, if you stopped to listen, everything prattled. It was a prattling world. Leaves as they tumbled in the breeze. Water as it went hopping over the stones and turned back on itself and hopped again. Cicadas that created such a long racketing shrillness, then suddenly cut out, so that you found yourself aware once again of silence. Except that it wasn't silence at all, it was a low, continuous rustling and buzzing and humming, as if each thing's presence was as much the sound it made as its shape, or the way it had, which was all its own, of moving or being still.

This old fellow his mule-driver, for instance, his Idaeus. What he had to say, his pleasant way of filling the time, was of no importance. It was full of something else. Interest.

It was as if you had found yourself peering through the crack in a door (exciting, Priam found, this imagining himself into a situation he would never have dreamed of acting out) and saw clearly for a moment into the fellow's life, his world – the world of the daughter-in-law too.

That matter of the little cakes, for instance. The ingredients that went into them, and the convenient device the man's son had come up with, out of simple affection, and to make things easier for the girl who was to cook them. It had never occurred to him that the food that came to his table so promptly, and in such abundance, might have *ingredients*. That a griddlecake or pikelet might have some previous form as batter. That batter might consist of good buckwheat flour and buttermilk, and that what you experienced as goodness might depend on the thickness of the batter or the light-ness of a wrist. Or that ingenious arrangements might need to be made before a thing as simple as a mere pikelet could make its entry into the world. Or that one of the activities a man might give his atten-tion to, and puzzle his wits over, was the managing of these arrangements, the putting together, in an experimental way, of this or that bit of an already existing world to make something new.

All that had been none of his concern. It had had no interest for him. Now it did. And he looked at the old fellow who had revealed these things to him with growing respect.

He knew things. The life he had come from, and had to some extent brought along with him, was full of activities and facts that, for all that they were common and low, had an appeal.

The good colour of the buttermilk, for instance, as it poured out of the crock: he liked what came to his senses when he pictured it. Even more the figure of the young woman as she squatted, her robe drawn up between her knees – but gracefully, modestly – to watch her cakes; flipping them over, very deftly so as not to burn her fingers, and when she did, popping the tips of them quickly into her mouth. All that was very lively and real. He could see it, though he had never seen *her*. And hadn't he tasted, in the one little cake he had popped into his own mouth, the lightness of the girl's wrist?

It had done him good, all that, body and spirit both. He wanted more.

To know, for example, whether that girl, the daughter-in-law, was well-favoured or not, and was meagre or on the plump side. How old was she? How did she dress her hair?

And the desire to fill out the picture, to see her more clearly, led to something very unaccustomed indeed, which he did not know how to deal with. The wish to put to the man one or two questions that were in no way necessary, served no purpose at all in fact, save the scratching of an itch he had discovered to know more about these unnecessary things, and to satisfy in himself a new sort of emptiness. Curiosity.

But the question, when he put it, was awkward, and did not touch on what he really wanted to know. It was a way, simply, of getting the fellow to start up again.

'So,' Priam said, 'you too have been blessed with sons.'

The man looked up.

'Blessed, my lord?' He shook his head. 'Well, you could say that. Blessed and then unblessed. In fact, sir, all I have left to me now is the daughter-in-law and a little girl four years old – no, she'll be four next month if the gods spare her – my grand-daughter. To tell the truth, sir, just at the moment she's a worry to me. If I've been a bit absent at times, and wrapped up in my own thoughts, it's because I've been thinking of her, poor soul, as you do, sir, when they are all that's left of your own blood. When I set out this morning she had a fever, and naturally I didn't expect then to be away for so long. By this hour most days I'd be home. Not that I mean to complain. But a fever is a worry. It's a terrible thing to see their little bodies all hot and tossing from side to side, and hear them gasping for breath. It seems like such a simple thing to a big strong fellow like me – a breath. You'd think you could just give it to them, free, even if it meant a little tightening in your own chest. It would be worth it, not to have the fear, the worry, you know, sir, of them being taken. But she's a strong little thing, there is that. Full of noise and mischief. Loves to be swung up on your shoulders and round and round till you're both dizzy. You should hear her scream. She's certainly got the breath for that! In just a few days, I dare say, she'll be running round the yard chasing the pigeons. But you worry just the same, it's in our nature. We're tied that way, all of us. Tied here,' and he closed his fist and brought it to his chest to indicate the heart.

'She fell once out in the yard, on a stake, and the blood that poured out you wouldn't credit in such a tiny creature. So much of it, and so red! All running away so fast I thought we'd never stop it. Then it stopped, just like that all on its own, as if something in her had said, "Enough, if things go on like this it'll be the end of me." What creatures we are, eh, sir? With so much life and will, and then, *pfff*, it's ended. Well, she opened her eyes, blinked at us, laughed, and for that time it was all over: just a good-sized scar that is still there on her forehead, you can't miss it. But we'd got a real fright, I can tell you. I shook all over. I thought, "I can't bear it, if anything happens to this little one, the last of my blood." I don't know what I'd have done if the gods hadn't thought again and been kind to us. But the truth is, we don't just lie down and die, do we, sir? We go on. For all our losses.

But I'd've been walking around, strong as I am, with a broken heart. My heart would have broken – it's near broke already. My wife, rest her spirit, gave me three sons and four daughters, and you know, sir, not one of them is still living.'

He sat with his shoulders slumped, shaking his head. 'Two of the boys got to be full-grown. The others, poor things, died early, of this and that. Stomach cramps, fits, fevers. One of the girls was so sickly she couldn't feed. It was lucky there was an older child, a boy, who could take the milk. My dear one's breasts swelled up like melons. They ached something terrible, and she cried and cried with the pain of it, though some of it was grief as well for the little one that just lay like a baby sparrow with its mouth open, gasping. Starved she was, too weak even to suck on your finger with a drop of milk on it. So the boy took it.'

Once again he moved away into his own thoughts and sat brooding. 'I can see him now. Such a lively little fellow. Laughing and wiping the milk from his mouth. He was too young, sir, to understand what it cost the other. He grew up all the stronger for it, but it's terrible to think of that little one's ghost out there, still wailing and unfed.

But there it is! The one was lost, the other prospered, grew up strong as a bull. There was no other fellow in the whole district hereabouts who could match him for wrestling, or hurling a log, or carrying a couple of sheafs on his back. The strength he had in his shoulders! The thickness of him! Of his neck. Like the trunk of one of those tamarisks.'

He paused again, and so long this time that Priam had to prompt him after a bit to go on.

'He's no longer living, you say?'

'That's right sir, he's not, he's not. In the end his strength was the death of him. A neighbour of ours, a careless, drunken fellow, had got his wagon bogged with a load of wood and the boy was helping him lift it. He crawled underneath, digging his way in under the shafts, all covered from head to foot in mud, and was trying to raise it on his back, arching and straining and sweating, when something burst, something in his innards. He let out such a cry, I can hear it now. Like nothing I've ever heard, sir, before or since. I break into a sweat myself, even now, just at the memory of it. The wagon tilted with the load and began to sink, with him under it. We had to dig him out. Half-drowned he was, in mud – in his mouth, choking him, in his eyes. All night he lay, white as your robe. Then blue, and that was the end of it.'

He sat shaking his head. 'Terrible. Terrible. To have got him up that far, and him so strong and likely to last it out. It leaves a gap you can't ignore. It's there. Always. The bit of a song he used to sing when he was washing out in the yard, preparing to go off with one of his girls. His cursing too, even that. And of course there was the work. Who was to take that on? It was hard on all of us. I sometimes think his mother died of it, poor soul. But he could be a difficult fellow at times. Light-headed, the way the young are sometimes. Foolish. He liked to show off. There was no reason for him to get under that wagon and do it all himself, except to show off in front of the rest. Though it was nothing in fact but a young lad's foolishness. He would have grown out of it in time, if they'd just have given him the chance. Maybe they regret it.'

He looked up, squinting a little. 'I knocked him down once, big as he was. I asked him to do something and he answered back with a why, and before I knew it I'd opened his lip with my fist. I've regretted it since. I've wished a thousand times over I'd just stood there and told myself, "He's young, he'll learn better, let it pass." Mightn't the gods regret it too, and think they acted too hasty, and be sorry now to have seen all that strength go for nothing in the world? Ah, there's many things we don't know, sir. The worst happens, and there, it's done. The fleas go on biting. The sun comes up again.'

The man fell silent, stared off into the distance, his features darkened by a look that twisted the mouth, hardened the jaw under its grizzled beard. He rubbed his nose with the heel of his hand.

Priam too sat silent. There was much to take in.

He too knew what it was to lose a son. He had lost so many in these last months and years, all of them dear to him – or so he had told himself.

He had stood beside the body of each one and poured wine from the cup and named him to the gods. Sent them, each one, lighted by smoking torches and accompanied by prayers and the formal wailing of women, down into the underworld. All as custom and the law demands. Fired the brand, set it to the pyre with its load of slaughtered oxen. Surely he of all men knew what it was to lose a son.

But when he considered the terms in which his companion had spoken, the lively manner, so full of emotion, in which he had called the boy up at the very moment of his raising the cart on the strong arch of his back, that cry, of a kind he had never heard before or since, when something broke in his innards; his singing as he washed out in the yard on his way to the girls – all that was so personal, and the man's memory of it so present and raw, even now in the telling of it, that Priam wondered if the phrase he had taken up so easily, that he knew what it was to lose a son, really did mean the same for him as it did for the driver. Whether what he had felt for the loss of Gorgythion, whose mother, the lovely Castianira, had come all the way from Aesyme to marry him, and Doryclus and Isus and Troilus and the rest, was in any way comparable to what this man had felt for a boy who was, after all, neither a prince nor a warrior, just a villager like so many more.

The truth was that none of his sons was in that sense particular. Their relationship to him was formal and symbolic, part of that dreamlike play before the gods and in the world's eye that is both the splendour and the ordeal of kingship. He could not even be sure of their actual number. Fifty, they said.

But that was only a manner of speaking, a good

round number. A bid, a powerful one, for the world's regard, an aggressive purchase on the future; clear evidence of a godlike activity in the sphere of breeding and begetting, another aspect of the necessary show. Like the list of his allies, or the measures of gold and the suits of embossed and finely worked armour, the cauldrons and tripods and precious cups that made up his fabled treasury. The *actual* number he could not swear to. Two or three more than fifty? Two or three less?

Of course he was in each case the source of their life, the forceful agent by which, in an onrush of manly desire, or out of habit or kingly duty, as he lay with Hecuba or with one of his many other wives and concubines, this or that prince had sprung into being.

The occasion itself was personal enough – none more so, the most personal of all. How else speak of that falling so pleasurably into the great dark, that sighing of the spirit into the very mouth of death, and in the midst of all, the rush of tender affection – for Hecuba, for instance, the first and dearest of his wives – and the sweet words that passed between them as they lay together afterwards; the hundred playful episodes in which they whisperingly teased and tempted one another. Like children themselves. Blessed, utterly blessed, and naked before the gods.

But as for the particular little offspring of so much high activity – his Isus, or Dius, or Troilus – well, he had no memory of any one of them as a three-year-old wiping the milk from his mouth, or sweating and racked with fever. He had never knocked any one of them to the ground and afterwards hugged his fist and regretted it. Such an act of violent intimacy was hardly within his comprehension. Nothing in the world he moved in would have permitted such a thing. Any more than he would have abandoned the austere stance he was constrained to by sweeping one of them up onto his shoulders and swinging round and round till the little body was limp with an excited shrieking.

Did he regret these human occasions, and the memory of them that might have twined his sons more deeply into his affections and made his relationship with them more warm and particular?

Perhaps.

But hadn't he been saved something as well?

When the years arrived in which, one after the other, his sons were brought in from the battlefield and he had twenty times over to stand by a corpse and pour out wine, and give the pierced and blood-less or hacked body a name, wouldn't he have suffered twenty times over if, as he held the brand to the pyre, he had had to remember how this one's sweat, when he crowned him once after a wrestling match, had had an odour of the stable as rank as any groom's; and how that one had had a little spinning top, and had fallen once when he went stumbling after it on the palace floor, and had recognised, with an unexpected onrush of recall, the star-shaped scar that was still visible on the young man's cheek, just inches from where a Greek javelin had shattered the jaw, smashed the teeth and taken a piece the size of his fist out of the back of his skull? Even the ghostly recollection now of what he had never in fact allowed himself to see made his old heart leap and flutter.

Royal custom – the habit of averting his gaze, always, from the unnecessary and particular – had saved him from all that. And yet it was just such unnecessary things in the old man's talk, occasions in which pain and pleasure were inextricably mixed, that so engaged and moved him.

'And the other?' he found himself asking,

almost before he was aware of it. 'You spoke of two sons.'

'Ah,' the man sighed. 'That happened only last spring, my lord. As chance would have it, not a hundred paces from here.'

He had taken up a stick and he threw it now far out into the stream. The fishlings, destined to be disappointed again, darted in towards the circles of light that went pulsing from where it fell, themselves for a moment making a small disturbance on the surface before the river went back to its own life again.

'There's another fording place down there. Not so easy as this one, but not difficult either if you know what you're about. Closer to the road. It was her fault, that little off-side mule I'm so fond of, Beauty, though I wonder at myself sometimes, she can be a bad-tempered creature if things don't suit her. She must have lost her footing halfway across. It was spring and the river was high and running fast over the gravel. He would have been trying to get her upright. She must have taken panic and knocked him sideways and they were both swept out into the stream.'

He rubbed his nose, as previously – it was,

Priam saw, a little habit with him – and sniffled. From off among the shadowy tamarisks came something like the hooting of an owl.

'We found him late the next morning – I'd been out all night looking for them – all tangled in the reeds on the other bank. And she, silly creature, she'd just walked out easy as you please and never looked back, and was grazing with her halter loose, in a patch of meadow-sweet. Switching her tail and pricking her ears when she caught sight of me.

'Of course she had no notion of what she'd done. But I was beside myself. I felt like punching her where she stood. But what would have been the good of that? That wouldn't have brought him back.

'I ended up taking her head in my arms and sobbing fit to break my heart. It was such a comfort just to hold on to her, and feel the warmth of her, and the scratchiness of her hide against my cheek. But whether it was for grief at my loss, or joy that she was safe, I can't tell you, sir. We're such contrary creatures. Maybe both. Anyway, since then I've been that fond of her, you wouldn't credit. She's all I've got left of him. Her and the daughter-in-law, and the little girl. I'm sorry, sir –' He lowered his head and brushed a rough hand across his eyes, and Priam, whose own eyes had moistened, looked away.

Almost imperceptibly while they were sitting dusk had come. 'My lord,' the carter said, 'it's getting dark, we should think of moving.'

He got slowly to his feet and, bending to dip his hand in the stream, splashed first his eyes, then his mouth and beard. Gathering up a fistful of his robe, he used it, rather delicately, to dab at his cheeks.

Priam looked about. It was true. A silvery greyness touched the river and the sandbars with their thickset bushes. The change had come quickly. Now that he was alerted to it, he saw that the river-colours were deepening, even as he watched, from blue-grey to a blackish purple.

He was sorry they had to move on. He had got used to the place and the small pleasures it provided, not least of all the opportunity to sit and listen to the other's talk. He would remember all this. The rosebay bushes with their long pointed leaves, that grew so strongly out of the sand and gravel between the streams. This cooling water that lapped his feet. The fishes. The high thin whining of the midges. There was a scent that seemed sharper now that other scents were fading with the sun – some herb. He would remember that too.

The carter was on his knees, folding his things in a neat bundle. When Priam stood and stepped out of the water, he produced a napkin and offered to dry the king's feet.

'That's the way, sir,' he coddled, as Priam, like a child, very placid and biddable, raised first his left, then his right foot to be dried, and when the driver indicated that he should resume his sandals, re-peated the action so that the man could fit them and fasten the cords. They set off then through the feathery pink tamarisks to where the cart and the tethered mules were waiting.

But they had advanced only a dozen paces when the carter, suddenly alert, laid his hand on Priam's arm and stayed him.

'Shhh,' he whispered, raising a minatory finger.

Leaning in a leisurely manner against the rails of the wagon, right foot crossed elegantly on the left, was a slim youth in a winged bonnet, below which his hair, which was of a burnished golden-bronze, hung in glossy ringlets. He was quietly absorbed, or so it seemed, in the contemplation of his own ladylike fingertips. Priam felt the pressure of the carter's hand on his forearm. His heart jumped.

The mules had already heard their approach or caught their scent. They turned, lifted their heads, and at the same moment, but languidly, the intruder also turned.

They saw then how young he was.

Idaeus, Priam observed, had his jaw set and was preparing to charge. The youth too must have perceived it. With a spring – all this on the instant – he was beside them, face contorted, short sword flashing.

'So what did you think, old fellow,' he was shouting, 'that I'd just let you jump and take me napping? I'm not a child, you know. Nor a thief either. Though if I'd wanted to nab your treasure – oh yes, I've taken a good look under the covers and seen the loot you're running off with – I could have walked away with anything I fancied in the half-hour you've been away dabbling your toes in the stream.'

Priam was confused. He knew something about anger, about angry *boys*, and this one was play-acting. His bluster was that of a youth who liked to hear his own voice and strike poses, which was not to say that he might not also be dangerous.

'Oh,' he said now, still full of swagger and noise, 'I suppose you're wary of me because I'm a Greek. No doubt you've heard all sorts of stories about what ruffians we are, what barbarians. Well look at me, do I look like a barbarian?'

It was true, he did not. With his rosy mouth and narrow waist and ringlets, he was very charming and knew it; charm was native to him. But so, if charm failed and these two old fellows he was making game of took offence or decided to turn courageous, was a suddenness in him that would cut them down without a second thought.

'The fact is,' the youth announced, 'I have been sent to be your escort,' and very chivalrously he brought his right hand to his bonnet, in a gesture – but it was only that – of doffing it, and inclined his pretty head.

'But I should introduce myself. My name is Orchilus. I am one of lord Achilles' men, one of his fearsome Myrmidons. Polyctor, my father is called, a rich man about the same age as yourself, sir –' he was addressing Priam. 'There were seven of us, seven sons. Only four are still living, of whom your servant here,' and he swept the bonnet from his head in an elegant flourish, 'is the youngest. So you see you have no reason, none at all, to be afraid for your lives, or even your treasure. Or to be, as I see you are, suspicious of my intentions. You are old, sir, and so, if he doesn't mind me mentioning it,' and he cast a glance in the carter's direction, 'is your noble companion. Suppose you were to run into a squad of pickets on night patrol, or two or three enterprising fellows who were out for a bit of fun – to find a girl or to steal a couple of chickens or a fat sheep – what a prize you'd make with all that booty under the coverlet! So, here I am at your service. Your guide and escort. Sent by the lord Achilles, who knows you are on the way, to protect you.'

This seemed strange. Priam acknowledged the youth's explanation but remained unconvinced. The fellow was just a little too good to be true.

The carter, he saw, was even more suspicious, and fearing the youth too might perceive it, Priam turned to his companion and said firmly, 'There, you see? We are in luck. The lord Achilles, in his great courtesy, has sent one of his squires to be our guide.'

'My lord,' the carter began – but Priam quickly cut him off.

'No, no,' he insisted, 'you heard what our young friend here has just told me. He has been sent.' (He caught the youth's smile, his look of half-mocking amusement.) 'So let us make ready and set off again.'

He was thinking of the punch the fellow had given his son and later regretted. He was concerned on the young stranger's behalf, but also on his own, lest the carter, believing he really had been fooled, should take matters into his own hands.

Meanwhile their unwanted companion had again taken up a lounging stance against the side of the cart. He yawned with what, to Priam, seemed studied indifference. All this fiddle-faddle, his eyebrow implied, was a hard test of a young fellow's patience.

But the carter was not so easily put off. Riled by the youth's impudence, his teasing condescension towards what he took, obviously, to be two bumbling oldsters (they had already set themselves at a disadvantage by getting ambushed, even if the ambush was for the moment a gentle one), he was determined to resist. He was the one who had got them into this pickle. He had allowed the king, and the treasure, and all that depended on it, to fall into the hands of a dandified puppy who, for all his oiled ringlets and languid lady-boy airs, was clearly a tough.

'We don't need an escort,' he told the youth bluntly. And under his breath, to Priam, 'My lord, we should shake this fellow off as quickly as we can. Thank him for his trouble, give him a nice silver cup, or a fancy pin for his cloak, and send him packing. Escort indeed! The first chance he gets he'll lead us into a ravine, and before we know it our throats will be cut.'

Priam cast a quick glance in the direction of their new friend, who again raised an eyebrow and shrugged, as if this sort of thinking was just what you might expect of a low fellow like a carter. Then he made a face as if to say, 'Your problem, my dear sir, don't expect *me* to get you out of it!' He really was a charmer.

Priam distrusted charm, especially when it took a physical form. He had learned a hard lesson on this point from his son Paris. But a sixth sense warned him that in this case something more might be involved than mere beauty and the lively self-assurance of youth. There was an unusual scent to the intruder's presence, though whether from his breath when he spoke, or from his body, was hard to tell. It was a fragrance of a kind Priam had never till now encountered. Some unguent or aromatic oil perhaps, with which the Greeks kneaded and eased their limbs after exercise, of a musky sweetness that if you were fighting at close quarters might be overpowering and hard to resist. And in fact Priam felt the intoxicating effect of it, even at a distance, a not-unpleasant yielding of his senses as the youth extended his hand and said, in a softer voice, 'Here, father, let me help you up. If we are to get to Achilles by suppertime we really must get going.'

Priam, a little surprised at how easily all this seemed to have been decided, allowed himself to be helped up into the cart.

'Come on, my man,' the youth called across to the driver, 'you're holding us up.' And the driver, seeing that the king had already submitted, went round to his side of the cart, spoke a word to his mules and, waving off the stranger's offer of a hand, hauled himself up, but with a spring to his step that was meant to indicate to His Impudence that he at least, despite his age, had no need of assistance and might be better able to defend himself than some people believed. The youth shrugged his shoulders and smiled.

Slowly they moved on down the bank to the crossing place, the young squire walking sometimes at the head of the wagon, beside the off-side mule, sometimes a step or two behind.

'Good day to you, little one,' he said very affably to the mule, and she, responsive as always to any sign of attention, lifted her pretty head and rolled an eye at him.

'Congratulations, old fellow,' he called back over his shoulder. 'I see your little sister here is one of the true servants of the gods.' He laid his hand on the mule's neck and tickled her softly behind the ear, and again she raised her head and responded. 'It makes me think the better of you.'

Does it indeed, the driver thought, and he started them off with a lurch. Little sister, is it? I thank you for that. I'll remember that!

He was furious. A good deal of it was jealousy. That his favourite had so immediately succumbed to the empty fellow's charms.

They had come to the water's edge, and the

driver halted now to let his mules take in what lay before them. Moonlight ran fast over the river pebbles. Ten paces beyond, where the channel deepened, the stream, with its many eddies, was moving thigh-deep in a rolling sweep.

They edged forward, the mules resisting. Priam felt the wheels grind against pebbles and slide a distance on the chalky bottom, then take a grip. The channel was running at one speed on the lighted surface but another, stronger current moved thickly below. Suddenly the cart lurched and tilted dangerously with its load. The wicker hood, when Priam's hand flew out to grasp it and steady himself, hung awry and seemed about to break loose.

The legs of the off-side mule had been caught by the force of the under-current, she was off her feet. Water, sluicing through the crescent-shaped openings in the wheels, had slewed the vehicle at a steep angle downstream. The whole outfit – mules, cart, its two helpless occupants, the load of treasure – were about to be pitched into the flood. Beside him Priam saw the carter rise unsteadily and prepare to leap in and attempt, hopeless though it might seem, to set them right. But the little mule was stronger and more self-possessed than she appeared. She propped, the wagon righted, and a moment later they were on firm gravel again with the water running easily round and past them; then, with shouts of encouragement from the driver and a vigorous heave, in the soft sand of the mid-stream island among shadowy bushes.

Their escort, though wet to the loins, had lost none of his cheery good humour. Having wandered downstream a little, 'It's safest down here,' he called back to the driver. He was crouched on his haunches about fifty paces off.

The driver, taking this as a challenge to his own judgement in these matters, ignored him. But when, after climbing down and making his own investigations, he got back into the cart and urged the mules forward, he turned them down to where the youth, on his feet again, was standing slim and dark against the glimmer of the second channel. Slowly they rolled down through yielding sand.

Again the mules resisted.

This second channel was deeper than the last. Water, suddenly high and swift-flowing, brimmed in tumultuous eddies round the wheels as the mid-stream current struck them. It rose again and was pouring now over the boards under their feet like the spill over a weir.

'An adventure, eh, father?' the youth shouted at Priam's elbow over the din made by the water. In to the waist now, he was wading strongly against it. 'You didn't expect this, eh, when you decided to set out?'

It was true, he had not. But here he was in the midst of it, and now that the first of his fear was past, he felt almost childishly pleased with himself. He was enjoying it. He hung on hard to the cross-bench and looked happily out over the expanse of sounding water with its eddies and haphazard cross-currents of light, already telling himself, in his head, the story of their crossing and feeling steadfast, even bold.

The bottom here was solid. For all the swirling around them of the icy stream, and the piled-up force of it against the body of the cart, they made good progress.

'Good work,' the driver shouted as they came within feet now of the bank; then, with water sluicing through the wheels, broke surface and struck the steepness of the rise. 'Just one more pull now,' he urged. 'Just one. Now, Beauty, *now*!' and he strained forward as if he could be a third beside them in the shafts.

The mules put their heads down, dug in with all the bunched strength of their hindquarters, and in just moments the wagon, Priam, the load and all were on dry land again. They were wet through, and as the wagon rolled on between low-growing maple scrub and sycamore figs and holm oak, water continued to drain away behind them, leaving muddy tracks. Meanwhile their escort had waded ashore, as easily as if water to him offered no more resistance than thin air. His tunic was soaked, but not a hair of his head was out of place and he showed not the smallest consequence of effort.

They came to a halt beyond the tree line. After the boisterous exertions and tumult of the crossing, there was only the sound now of their breathing in the muted stillness, and again the *woo-wooing* from far off of an owl. The expanse of open land before them was patched with shadow in some places, lighted in others by an early moon.

The driver, with his usual diligence, got down and inspected the cart, front and back, to see that all was well. Then, remounting, he led the mules this way and that till he felt the beginnings of a road under the wheels. Only then did he speak.

'Well, that wasn't so bad,' he opined. 'It's a straight road from here on. Well done, Beauty! Well done, Shock!'

The mules, still glossy-wet from their ducking, responded and began to trot.

The moon was rising fast now. Soon, wafer-like and as if lit from within, it stood high over what had, till the war laid waste to them, been standing wheat fields and groves of ancient olives.

Priam sat silent. Till now he had seen nothing of this.

The landscape they were entering was one of utter devastation. Little starveling bushes sprouted from the dust, and all across the plain small squirrel-like creatures that had been gnawing at the slender stems sat up on their haunches to stare at them, noses trembling, then, with a scurry, dropped from sight into holes in the earth. In the windless sky big clouds edged with silver stood still before the stars: Orion, the Twins, the Pleiades, misty-white in their net.

After a little, their escort, who could not long keep silent, resumed his chatter, every now and then enquiring after Priam's royal comfort and at last, after another silence in which he might finally have run out of talk, asked very pleasantly of the carter: 'And that pretty daughter-in-law of yours? How is she? Still troubled, poor girl, by her limp?'

The carter hid his astonishment with a narrow-eyed glare. What cheek!

And how could the fellow know of her? He felt a pang of unease, but also a faint glimmering of something else that was gone before he could grasp it. He hunched into himself and pretended not to have heard.

Priam too was surprised. The driver had not mentioned a limp. It formed no part of the picture he had fashioned of the young woman as she squatted beside hot stones, flipping pancakes with the tips of her fingers, and if they were too hot, popping her fingers into her mouth. He would have to begin all over again, though he was glad to hear that she was pretty.

'Ah,' the youth said, 'I can see you're not pleased, old fellow, that I know so much about you. But I know more than that. A lot more!' and he gave a teasing laugh. 'I know you've got a temper for instance and are on the sly side, that you're a rogue in fact. I don't say an outright scoundrel, but a fellow who's not too particular about the law. Fond of the tavern too. Isn't that what they say of you? A bit of a tippler, and a storyteller and spinner of tales. I know you pretty well, eh?' And he cocked his head in a disingenuous, frankly disarming way and laughed again.

The carter was casting little sideways glances at Priam. He was sorry the king should have to hear this low gossip about him. He could have knocked the fellow to the ground, with his scurrilous talk and his air of being so pleased with his own cleverness. But something restrained him. Some inkling that all here was not quite as it seemed. That he had best keep an eye out and hold back.

'Well,' the youth said lightly, 'the gods bless you. To tell the truth, I'm not too particular myself when it comes to the law, so I won't hold that against you. And it's a good thing to be merry and like a joke. You do, don't you, like a joke?' But the carter was glaring. 'Well, maybe I've gone too far. I'll stop chattering, old fellow, if all it does is get your temper up. But I'm young, you know. My head is full of this, that and I don't know what, and the world is such a lively and interesting place that I can't help getting carried away. And it's a tempting thing when you're young as I am to talk and hear news of all that's happening in the world. Time enough later to be long-faced and glum, and sit still, and go *hem* and *hum*. We're a long time in the earth, father. Plenty of silence there.'

'Sir,' the driver whispered aside to Priam, who was sitting straight on the crossbench, his figure as wooden as the bench itself, 'sir – this fellow who is with us – I know he's wearing a Greek bonnet and is dressed like one, but I wonder if he really is a Greek. Or even, my lord –' and he lowered his voice still further – 'a man like the rest of us.'

'What's that, old fellow?' the youth demanded from the off-side of the cart, and the little mule turned her head at the change in his voice, which was no longer light and youthful like that of her friendly stranger. 'What are you mumbling there? I've got good ears, you know, it's no use whispering. So you think I'm not a man like the rest of you, is that it? What am I then? *Who* am I?'

Priam's eyes opened wide. He wondered how he had not seen it before. 'My lord,' he breathed. 'My lord Hermes!'

The carter too was wide-eyed. With his usual feigned indisposition to be astonished by anything the world might throw at him, he disguised the alarm he felt, but could not avoid asking himself one or two discomforting questions.

If he really was the celestial joker – messenger, thief, trickster, escort of souls to the underworld – where were they heading? Had they drowned back there, when he had led them so cheerfully to his chosen crossing place? Were they already disembodied souls on their way to the afterlife?

He pinched himself. Didn't feel like it! Pushed his nose into the yoke of his robe and sniffed. Didn't smell like it either.

'I see you are amazed,' the god said, 'both of you. Well, that is understandable, and proper too. What I told you is true, I *was* sent. Though not by Achilles, who knows nothing of your coming.'

He saw the look of alarm that passed between the two. That too was understandable and he hastened to reassure them.

'Sent, yes, but not for the usual reasons, nothing of that sort is intended. Not on this occasion. The next time you see me will be a different story. But you'll know me then, won't you, old fellow? I am, by the way,' and he paused to take his gloves from his belt and draw them very delicately over his slender fingertips, 'invisible, though *you* can see me well enough. Oh, and that little girl you have been so concerned about –' this to the carter, as if he had just called it to mind – 'she's sitting up now eating a bowl of barley porridge and asking where you've got to and when you'll be back.' He turned, addressing the king. 'Now, father,' he said gravely, 'the time has come to gather your strength. The Greek trench is just beyond that second barrow. We're almost there.'

Priam found himself suddenly overcome. He was at the limit of his strength. The moment had arrived when he must do in fact what to this point he had done only in plan, in the realm of thought. Would he be equal to it? Faint with weakness at the thought of coming face to face at last with Achilles, he felt his eyelids droop, as if he might be about to seek refuge in sleep.

What strengthened him was the presence at his side of his good Idaeus, who seemed in no way intimidated by their escort's transformation. As if the arrival of a god on the scene was in his life a quite ordinary occurrence, one more eventuality to be recognised and taken account of in a world of endless surprise and accident.

Perhaps it was bravado. A determination not to be impressed, or at least not to show it. If so, it worked, it had its effect, and he too felt the benefit.

He took comfort as well from the title the god had just given him. The youth had addressed him as father on earlier occasions, but Priam had taken it then as no more than another aspect of his playful teasing, the sort of half-affectionate, half-patronising tone that young men adopt, especially young men who are in love with their own importance, when they are dealing with the old. Respectful yes, ingratiating even, but with a hint as well of amused condescension. Now, with the play about to begin in which he was to represent 'the father' – and in a way he had never till now attempted – he was moved by this invocation of the sacred tie, and took it, from a god's lips, as an endorsement and blessing.

The youth – Hermes – clasped his wrist, and Priam felt a jolt as his blood responded to the firm, rather icy touch. Then a slow energy flooded his limbs.

They had arrived at the trench before the stockade wall. Two body-lengths wide, three

sword-lengths deep, it was overgrown with this-
tles and protected by a hedge of sharpened stakes
set at a forward angle.

Beyond it, twelve feet high and made of pine
logs caulked with oakum, was the high portal gate
to the camp. Three men were needed to raise the
pine trunk with which it was barred. Only Achilles
among mortal men could manage it alone.

A company of Argives was on duty in the inner
yard. Scattered across the open space, they were
squatting round the embers of cookfires where
their evening meal was broiling, or sprawled on
their cloaks playing at dice. It was the early
watch, an easy hour. When a sudden knocking
came at the gate the captain of the guard looked
up surprised. No signal had come in from the
pickets he had posted of strangers approaching
the camp.

He climbed slowly to his feet and, with two or
three men at his side, started out across the yard.
The others, or as many of them as were not too

deeply absorbed in talk or in their dice-games, looked on in a casual way to see what was amiss.

But the captain and his companions had barely advanced a dozen paces when, with a *crack!* that brought the whole yard to its feet, the massive pole that barred the gate, as if moved by some invisible agency, broke from its crutch and slowly began to rise.

The captain and his companions stood as if spellbound, the hands on their half-drawn swords too heavy to lift, the tongues in their open mouths also stopped, and their feet, their breath.

Slowly, as they watched, the leaves of the gate creaked on their hinges and swung open.

A covered wagon was there, five paces outside the gate, drawn by two black mules and with two old men seated side by side on the crossbench.

Only when it had lurched and rumbled on into the camp, and the leaves of the great gate had closed behind it, and the bar, once again as if moved by invisible hands, had dropped with a thud into its lock, did the watchers, all staring now, give voice to their consternation, each man doubting what he had seen.

Achilles is at mess in his hut. He eats almost nothing these days but feels obliged out of consideration for his men to make an appearance.

The men, all closely crowded shoulder to shoulder, share a trestle table in the centre of the hut. Achilles sits apart, at a little folding table of inlaid ivory that his attendants, Automedon and his squire Alcimus, have set in a secluded corner where the torchlight does not reach.

Under the low thatched roof the air is thick with the smell of pitch from pinewood torches that sputter and pour out smoke and acrid fumes; and of animal fat and the sweat of unwashed bodies. The men are noisy. The noise they make gathers to an uproar, then lapses, then rises again, wave on wave, like the sea. Cups are banged down hard in drunken fists.

A quarrel breaks out. A shaggy head above a shaggier fur-clad shoulder looms in giant reflection against the flickering red of the deal-plank wall. Others leap to join it, and for a time they surge in lumbering shadow play, from which sweaty faces, wet mouths, black eye-pits, flare, half-dark, half-flame. Then the heave subsides, and the big shadows go back to being the solid bodies of men, who slap one another on the back and, shouting, crowd in close, shoulder to shoulder. In a quiet moment someone begins a rambling reminiscence, some old sadness or talk of home, and is roughly silenced. More wine is carried in.

Achilles barely notices all this. It is just the noise that grown men make when they are in company and afraid of where silence might take them. Trees in a blow make such a din. So do stones when they dash together.

He sits with a full cup of wine before him, eating only so that his attendants will be free to eat.

Now that Patroclus is gone, Automedon is his chief attendant, the driver of his chariot and his close body-servant. One of the noblest of the Myr-midons, he is a lean-jawed fellow of an impressive lankness, with eyes deep-set and reflective under thickset brows. What is happening around him seems never entirely within his grasp. He is in consequence the most cautious and reliable of men, doing all he does with perfect consideration and punctilious rectitude. But Achilles is not quite easy with him. He admires the man but is not drawn to him, as Patroclus was.

The fact is, he resents Automedon. His presence is both a reminder and a rebuke.

When the helmet was struck from Patroclus' head and he went reeling, hot blood gushing from his mouth, it was this man, Automedon, who ran to lift him up, and holding him close in his arms, watched the light that moved cloudlike across his gaze as the bright world dimmed, and crying out and leaning closer, caught the last breath at his lips. It was Automedon who stood astride the body and, blinded by tears, fought the Trojan jackals off.

Him, Achilles tells himself bitterly, not me. In his arms, not mine.

It is because he resents Automedon that Achilles has made him his squire. Patroclus, he knows, would expect nothing less of him. But the thought is there, always. Him, not me – and it rankles.

Automedon, alert to every mood in Achilles, is aware of this. He recognises Achilles' grief; he too is grieving. He loves the man, and not only for Patroclus' sake, and does not let the hurt he feels affect the attention he gives to even the smallest and most unspoken of Achilles' needs. Ever watchful, when Achilles gives the sign at last, he nods to Alcimus and they draw stools up to the table and join him.

They are young, these men, and have hearty appetites. Forcing himself, Achilles takes something from each of the dishes they have set before him – scallions, a handful of olives, bread, a little sour cheese. The wine they have mixed and poured he barely touches.

Automedon tries not to make it obvious that they have been holding back. But Alcimus, who is just a boy, does not. When Achilles has served himself, his big hands go quickly to the platter of roast meat, the bread in its woven basket, and his jaws work horribly over the gobbets of fat.

Automedon, Achilles observes, says nothing. He does not have to. Suddenly conscious of the sound his chewing makes, Alcimus swallows the last pieces whole, and when he sucks the grease from his fingers it is in a restrained, maidenly way that is almost comic.

Achilles is fond of Alcimus and feels sorry for him. He would rather, he knows, be with the others, banging his cup down on the trestle table and tearing at his food as he shouts to be heard above the crowd. It is this overabundance in him of an animal nature he has not yet learned to subdue that Achilles finds endearing in the youth, and which makes his lapses into hulking awkwardness so easy to forgive. He likes to have Alcimus by him. For his own sake, but as a reminder too of what he himself was just a season ago.

Once again he reaches into a dish so that his companions can seize the occasion and do likewise. Takes a skewer of meat. Turns it in his fingers. Puts it back.

Now, in the smoky darkness at the far end of the hut, a hand sweeps across sounding strings. Achilles raises his head.

A god moves invisible among them, and in the wake of his passing the full-throated shouting of the Myrmidons is cut off. The silvery notes of the lyre touch and change the air. When the voices start up again, as they do soon enough, they are not so loud that the music cannot be heard beneath them. It persists. And so, for Achilles, does the chord the music has struck in him.

He knows what this sudden suspension of his hard, manly qualities denotes. This melting in him of will, of self. Under its aspect things continue to be just themselves, but what is apprehensible to him now is a fluidity in them that on other occasions is obscured. The particles of which they are composed, within the solid forms, tumble and swarm. As if flow, not fixity, were their nature. The world swims, and for as long as the mood lasts he too is afloat.

He has moved into his mother's element and is open again to her shimmering influence. In such moods he *sees things* – a thickening of the half-light beyond Automedon's shoulder that strikes him first as a startling of his blood.

A figure, as yet all hovering vagueness, has begun to take shape there.

Patroclus, he breathes. You! At last, at last! He watches spell-struck as the figure advances through the smoky dark towards him.

But this is no young man. His disappointment dissolves in another, deeper sorrow.

The figure, tall, spare, wearing a white robe without decoration, is old. The loose flesh under the chin hangs in wrinkled folds, the eyes deep-set under knotty brows.

Father?

It is half a question this time. Slowly he rises from his seat.

Alcimus glances at Automedon, then back across his shoulder to see what is there. He sees, and he and Automedon start up both and reach for their swords. Achilles, half-risen, continues to stare.

It is nine years since Achilles last saw his father. When he sailed from Phthia he was little more than a boy, already fully grown and well-made but with few signs upon him of the man he has become – a warrior, deep-chested, thick in the shoulders and neck, his features roughened by long months of bivouacking on the open plain. It is what time has done to him. And it strikes him now, in a great wave of sadness, how much his father too is changed.

The Peleus he left, who had clasped him so

strongly to his breast, reluctant to the point of tears to let him go, had been in the prime of life, strong-thewed and warrior-like, a man to be feared. The figure who comes to him now is still noble-looking and tall, but all his muscles are slack. The hair, once thick and iron-grey, is thin and of a fleecy whiteness.

'Father,' he says again, aloud this time, over-come with tenderness for this old man and his trembling frailty. 'Peleus! Father!'

The great Achilles, eyes aswarm, is weeping. With a cry he falls on one knee, and leans out to clasp his father's robe. Automedon and Alcimus, their swords now drawn and gleaming, leap to his side.

'Sir!'

Achilles, startled, looks again.

The man is a stranger. Noble, yes, even in his plain robe, but not at all like Peleus. What tricks the heart can play! The man is clearly not his father, but for half a hundred beats of his heart his father had been truly present to him, and he con-tinues now to feel tenderly vulnerable to all those emotions in him that belong to the sacred bond.

Which is why, to the puzzlement of his two

attendants, he does not immediately take the interloper by the throat but enquires, almost mildly, 'But who are you? How did you get into this hut?' As if, whoever he might be, there was something uncanny in this stranger's appearing so suddenly, and unnoticed, in a place thick with his followers.

The old man totters and looks as if he might fall. He glances apprehensively at the younger of the two men who face him with drawn swords. Alcimus, lionlike, can barely restrain himself from springing.

Achilles, seeing what it is that has alarmed the man, makes a sign, and Alcimus, after a quick look to Automedon for confirmation, sheathes his sword.

Priam steadies himself. The occasion has moved too quickly, and in a way he is not prepared for. He has come here to kneel to Achilles. Instead the great Achilles is kneeling to him. Still, the moment has arrived. He must go on.

'I am Priam, King of Troy,' he says simply. 'I have come to you, Achilles, just as you see me, just as I am, to ask you, man to man, as a father, for the body of my son. To ransom and bring him home.'

Priam closes his eyes. Now, he thinks. Now, they will strike.

The two attendants continue to stand alert, Automedon still hand on sword. Achilles rises to his feet. But nothing happens.

'But how did you get here?' he asks. 'Into the camp? Into this hut?'

'I was guided,' Priam answers. And in recalling the god who has led him here, Hermes the giant-killer, he takes heart.

Achilles, he sees, is impressed by this. He does not repeat the word but it is registered in the line that appears between his brows, the slight parting of his lips. He understands immediately, Priam sees, that more than ordinary forces have brought him here. Despite the vast bulk of the man, the span of the shoulders, the ropelike muscles of the neck, the warrior in him has, for the moment at least, been subdued.

'I came in a wagon,' he explains. 'With my herald, Idaeus. He is out there in the yard with the treasure I have brought you.'

He does not kneel. The occasion for that has passed. So the whole scene, as he had imagined and acted it out in his mind, does not take place.

Instead, he stands quietly in the stillness that surrounds them, despite the noise that Achilles' Myrmidons are making, and waits.

Achilles narrows his eyes, examines the man before him. He makes a sign, almost invisible, to Automedon, who removes his hand from his weapon and goes out.

All this has happened so quickly and so quietly in this darkened corner of the hut that the men at the big mess table remain unaware of the extraordinary happening in their midst. They continue to shout one another down in boisterous argument and raise their cups in drunken toasts. Under the din they make, the notes of the lyre continue to colour the air. All of which gives the moment, as Achilles experiences it, a dreamlike quality.

The tenderness of his earlier mood is still strong upon him. Beyond this old man who claims – can it be true? – to be Priam, King of Troy, hovers the figure of his father, which is too immediate in Achilles' mind, too disturbing, to be pushed aside. Impatient to know what it is exactly that he has to deal with, he makes a sign to Alcimus to go after Automedon and bring back news of what he has found.

But Alcimus, reluctant to leave his master alone, hesitates, and before he can make the move, Automedon is back. He is bundling in a second old man, sturdier than the first. Shock-headed and dressed in a garment of coarse homespun, he bears no resemblance at all to the Trojan herald, whom Achilles has seen on at least three previous occasions in the camp.

'It's true,' Automedon reports in a whisper, 'there is a wagon loaded with treasure. In fact, sir,' and he lowers his voice even further, 'it's just an ordinary hay-wain. This fellow is the driver of it. Rather odd, I'd say, and argumentative. He did not want to leave his mules.'

'You are Idaeus, the king's herald?' Achilles asks the man. He is puzzled. Not simply by the claim that this rough-looking fellow should be Priam's herald but by a situation that has already passed beyond anything he has a precedent for. What surprises him is how easy he feels, despite Automedon's warning.

The carter, who is rather alarmed in fact at being brought into this business, and by the smoky darkness of the place, and the noise, which is more like what you would expect of a tavern than of a hero's camp, rubs his nose, a gesture that serves to settle him, and scratches his head. He is playing for time. Now that the question has been put, so directly and with Priam looking on, he does not see how he can answer.

'Well, old fellow,' Achilles asks again, 'you are the famous Idaeus?'

Idaeus?

He isn't – of course he isn't, he's Somax. A simple workman, who this morning, as on every other morning of his life, just happened to be standing in the marketplace waiting to be hired when two strangers appeared who just happened to be the king's sons, Trojan princes. One of whom came to a halt, and with a nod in his direction tugged lightly at the other's sleeve, instantly attracted, as people often were, to the little off-side mule, his famous Beauty – all of which, though true enough and relevant, at least to himself, does not even begin to account for the unlikeliness of all this. The words to cover it are there in his head but would get turned about and jumbled if he tried to get them out. And how can he explain, with Priam there to hear it, that this king who is in his care, for all his grave authority, is as innocent of the world as a naked newborn babe, and just as helpless?

What he does say is: 'If you please, sir, Idaeus is the name they have given me. Because the king's helper is always called that. Idaeus. And the king's . . . helper, today' (he had almost forgotten himself and said 'companion') 'happens to be me. The cart and the mules, sir, are mine. The treasure I was guarding . . .'

But he does not know what to say of the treasure, or to whom at this point it rightfully belongs.

Fortunately Priam sees the difficulty he is in and intervenes.

'Achilles, I called this man my herald because I am by ancient custom used to having a herald to drive my chariot, and also, if needed, to speak for me. On this occasion I mean to speak for myself, but this good man has come along to drive the wagon with the treasure I am bringing. He is a carter – no need to dress things up by calling him more. It would be a great courtesy to me if you did not ask too much of him,' and Priam, turning away from Achilles, addresses the carter. 'You have done me good service,' he tells the man. 'I could not have asked for better. Whatever happens here, I thank you for it, and if all goes well will see you are rewarded. I should be very sorry if any harm came to you on my account. But in that we are in other hands. Both of us.'

Priam is deeply moved. So is his companion, who rubs his nose, keeps his eyes on the ground, and makes little deprecatory gestures that suggest he has in fact done very little.

Achilles is intrigued by this by-play between the two old men, who belong to such different worlds – the humility of the one, the awkward shyness of the other – and all the more because it has proceeded as if it were a matter strictly between the two of them and he had no place here. He might have taken offence at this, but for some reason he does not. The unfamiliarity of it, the unlikeliness, takes him out of himself. It amuses him.

'Alcimus,' he says, 'take this good fellow out and see that he is fed. Let him have feed as well for his mules.'

Alcimus steps forward to escort the carter out, and Priam, under the influence of what he has just said, and the quietness with which Achilles has received it, feels emboldened after a moment to go on. 'Achilles,' he begins, 'I appeal to you as a father –'

He pauses, and Achilles, who is prepared for this, stands ready to hear the old man out. But what Priam says now catches him entirely off guard.

'You are, I know, the father of a son you have not seen for more than half his lifetime. A boy growing up in his grandfather's house in far-off Scyros. Think what it would mean to you, Achilles, if it was his body that was lying out there, unconsecrated after eleven days and nights in the dust. The body of a son for whom you have a father's soft affections, to whom you owe sacred duties that nothing, nothing in the world, can cancel. Do you think I ever imagined, when I was a young man as you are now, in the pride and vigour of my youth, that I would in old age come to this? To stand, as I do now, undefended before you, and with no sign about me of my royal dignity, begging you, Achilles – as a father, and as one poor mortal to another – to accept the ransom I bring and give me back the body of my son. Not because these cups and other trifles are a proper equivalent – how could they be? – or for any value you may set upon them. But because it does high honour to both of us to act as our fathers and forefathers have done through all the ages and show that we are men, children of the gods, not ravening beasts. I beg you, ask no more of me. Accept the ransom and let me gather up at last what is left of my son.' And the old man turns away, unable to go on.

Achilles frowns, sinks into himself. Priam's evocation of the boy Neoptolemus has touched a sore spot whose ache he has long suppressed.

Nine years ago, when he last saw him, Neoptolemus was a mere child, a sturdy seven-year-old, boisterous and proud, with flamy red-gold hair and a saddle of freckles across his nose; an impish small man with the swagger and gruffness of voice, and a brow stern enough for a veteran of forty, that children of that age, in mimicry of their elders, will assume at times with an almost comic effect.

And now?

He has tried to picture the grown youth of sixteen, hard-bodied and full of manly resolution, already eager to prove himself, already urging his grandfather, Lycomedes, to let him leave his tutors and the exercise of the palaestra and set sail for

Troy, and take his place at last at his father's side as one of his fearsome Myrmidons. But haunted as he is by old affection, it is the swaggering child who leaps into his mind. All Achilles can see when he looks back across those nine years is the small mimic hero, striding up and down in his grandfather's hall and posturing with his miniature sword and scowl and little-mannish antic bluster.

But Priam has recovered.

'Achilles,' he says, his voice steady now, 'you know, as I do, what we men are. We are mortals, not gods. We die. Death is in our nature. Without that fee paid in advance, the world does not come to us. That is the hard bargain life makes with us – with all of us, every one – and the condition we share. And for that reason, if for no other, we should have pity for one another's losses. For the sorrows that must come sooner or later to each one of us, in a world we enter only on mortal terms. Think, Achilles. Think of your son, Neoptolemus. Would you not do for him what I am doing here for Hector? Would your father, Peleus, not do the same for you? Strip himself of all the ornaments of power, and with no concern any longer for pride or distinction, do what is most human – come as I do, a plain man white-haired and old, and entreat the killer of his son, with whatever small dignity is left him, to remember his own death, and the death of his father, and do as these things are honourably done among us, to take the ransom I bring and give me back my son.'

In the stillness that follows – for the noise his men are making no longer comes to his ears – Achilles feels immobilised and outside time.

This morning, on the beach beyond the line of Achaean ships, he had stood staring out across the gulf and felt that it was not space his mind was being drawn into, but the vast expanse of time, at once immediate in the instant and boundless, without end.

Now, in the aftermath of Priam's words, he sees beyond Priam another old man, both closer and further off: his father Peleus, and beyond him another, himself, the old man he will never be. And is struck, in a breath and in all his limbs, by such a coldness as he has never known, even on the deepest winter nights on the Trojan plain. Ice ribs him round with an iron grip. It is the coldness of that distant star that is the body's isolation in death.

The moment passes, the thick ice cracks. In his return to the heat and noise of the hut his eyes burn so that he has to cover them with his hand. When he looks up again there is, around everything he sees – the old man Priam who stands before him, the mob at the trestle table – a reddish glow, as if his eyeballs were awash with blood. A fireball comes whistling through the air, a fiery-headed agent of such destructiveness as all these nine years of slaughter have not seen. Priam, in evoking his own death, has let in among them the fearsome instrument of it. Achilles feels the breath of a hot sword in the air. Sees, as through a momentary opening in eternity, the old man Priam go sprawling. Hears the armed Fury, in a burning glance across his shoulder, shout into the dark: 'There, father! There, Achilles! You are avenged.'

Achilles sits soul-struck. It is his son, Neoptolemus.

What he has witnessed, in the illumination of the moment as Priam has called it up, is a time to come, the end of things in the days after his death.

Priam, impelled by the look of annihilating revelation that has struck the man, falls to his knees at last and clasps Achilles' hands. Not in supplication now, as he had intended, but out of instant fellow-feeling.

So the scene is acted after all.

But Achilles mistakes the gesture for more pleading. With a look of horror he starts back and roughly pushes the old man off.

'No,' he shouts, 'no more!' and his voice is raw with anguish. 'Don't speak again. You will have what you came for.'

He ignores the sob that comes from the old man and rejects the attempt to clasp his knees.

'No more! Please! When Hector's body has been washed and prepared, we will eat something together and you can rest. Till then, my attendants will see to you.' And he offers the man, who seems suddenly too weak to get up without assistance, his hand.

So Achilles, as he has done each morning now for eleven days, goes down to where the body of Hector lies in the dust.

Automedon, torch in hand, goes with him. A groom follows with a folding stool under his arm and a stake with an iron bracket.

It is an hour before midnight. A breeze has cleared the sky of cloud, and the stars, some huge and single, others in shoals or clusters, hang so low that Achilles believes he can smell them, the air out here is so fresh and clean after the smokiness of the hut.

Automedon fixes the torch in its bracket. The groom unfolds the stool, drives its legs into the soft earth, tests it for balance. Achilles nods. Automedon and the groom may leave now. He wants to be alone. But Automedon, who is a worrier, hesitates.

'No,' Achilles tells him. 'Go now. I'll call when I need you.'

Automedon has no recourse but to obey.

Achilles, alone at last with his thoughts, draws his cloak about him and sits.

At his feet the body of his dead enemy. It shines as with the light of another star, a metallic brightness. Except for the wound at the throat where his sword went in, it is unmarked. The wound is as clean as if it had just been made. After eleven days in the sun the body has neither the discolouration nor the smell of corruption.

Achilles sits and contemplates it: shining brow, lean jaw, the cheeks sunken a little. On the upper lip and chin just the shadow of a beard.

Each morning, when he rides down to confront it, this is what he finds, this figure of what might be a sleeper, composed and still in the naked perfection of its early manhood, laid out as a challenge to him, from the gods, to inflict upon it – the body of the slayer of his friend – the savage depredations that his pride, his grief, his sense of his own high honour demand, and which the spirit of Patroclus, if love is to prove itself, must witness. And each morning, when he discovers yet again how the gods have defied him, he is maddened anew. Outrageous injury swells his veins.

And now?

Leaning forward on the stool, he once again examines his enemy. Frowns. Raises his brow to the clear night sky. Breathes in its freshness.

Something in him has freed itself and fallen away. A need, an obligation. Everything around him is subtly changed. The body at his feet, in the rightness of its imperturbable calm, his own body, which is tensed as it tips forward, also calm. Some cleansing emotion that flooded through him – when? – when Priam first appeared to him in the figure of his father? – has cleared his heart of the smoky poison that clogged and thickened its every motion so that whatever he turned his gaze on was clouded and dark.

He regards Hector's body now, and the clean-limbed perfection of it, the splendour of the warrior who has won an honourable death, is no longer an affront.

The affection of the gods for a man whose end it was part of his own accomplished life to accomplish he can now take as an honour intended also to himself. And that, he sees, is how it might have been from the start, and this the first, not the twelfth night.

What he feels in himself as a perfect order of body, heart, occasion, is the enactment, under the stars, in the very breath of the gods, of the true Achilles, the one he has come all this way to find.

He sits quietly in the contemplation of this.

The light of the torch casts a flickering glow a little upwards into the air, creating an effect, in the dark, of a cave whose roof is also the high roof of his skull. At his feet, the body whose quiet he can accept now as a mirror of his own. So long as he sits here, there can be no conflict between them. They are in perfect amity. Their part in the long war is at an end.

So he sits. Then, with a last look down, rises and calls into the dark to where Automedon, just a little way off, has all this time been waiting and keeping watch.

Two grooms carry Hector's body, slung in a clean sheet, into the low-ceilinged laundry hut. Achilles, stooping, watches as they lay their burden on a scrubbed tabletop, then bob their heads and go out at the low door.

Steam from a cauldron thickens the air, and sharp-smelling woodsmoke. On a bench against the slab wall, an oil crock, a dish with herbs. Beside them, smoothly folded, the linen in which, when it has been sponged and anointed, Hector's body will be wrapped.

The women who have been woken and called in

to do all this, black-shawled and with heavy large-pored faces, huddle in the shadows. Achilles' presence makes them uncomfortable. The work they do here is women's work – common enough, they do it daily, but not for the eyes of men. They are waiting for him to leave before they will begin.

But Achilles, who has never before been to this hut, and has never till now even considered its existence, is intrigued. Having followed Hector's body this far, he is curious to see the next stage of its passage into extinction: the business, humble but necessary, of its last commerce with the world in the hands of women.

And the place itself, now that he has discovered it, compels him in a way he cannot at first account for. There is something here, something about the atmosphere of the place, the damp sweet laundry smell, that he half-recalls and recognises. A room in his father's palace where he was taken sometimes in the arms of his nurse, whose skin, close up, was large-pored like the skin of these laundry women and whose damp hair he can feel against his cheek. Suddenly he is there again – that smell of dried herbs cut with lye; they have come to fetch a bedsheet for his afternoon nap.

This is the first world we come into, he thinks now, this world of hot-water pitchers and oil jars and freshly laundered linen or wool. And the last place we pass through before our body is done with it all. Unheroic thoughts.

Stooped a little, and still closely wrapped in his cloak, he remains standing, awkward and out of place, just inside the door.

Hector's body, naked now but with a corner of the sheet drawn lightly over the thighs – a gesture towards modesty on the part of one of the grooms – lies outstretched and waiting, its flesh made rosy by the torchlight, the feet turned out a little. Drawn once again by the deep abstraction of its calm, which his own still feeds on, Achilles is unwilling to break away.

But the women's presence is stronger than his own. This is their world. So long as he stands here watching they will not begin. He turns, ducks his head under the low door, and steps out again into the yard.

Starlight, shadows, the figures of young men, his Myrmidons on duty. The metal of their swords glinting as they move about between the fires. Bodies sinewy, taut, ready for hard use. Out here, for a time yet, he is one of them; the air, with its cool edge, a reminder of how present and warm he is in his envelope of flesh.

For a time.

Till he too, like Hector, is in there. Naked as he began. Being turned this way then that in the hands of women.

First light. A powdering of frost on the ground. In the portico of Achilles' hut, where they have made a bed for him of rugs spread with a fine linen sheet, Priam is still sleeping, stiff and straight under two woollen blankets drawn close under his chin. Achilles, watching, is touched by the old man's dignity, even in sleep, and his thoughts fly once again to Phthia and his father Peleus. The chin is lifted just above the selvedge of the blanket, which is purple, bordered with gold. As the breath blows through them, the lips make a puffing sound, then narrow as a new breath is drawn in.

'Priam. Priam.' Achilles bends down towards the sleeping face. 'It is time.'

The eyes click open and for a heartbeat there is panic in their gaze. The mouth opens, the cheeks are sucked in. Then the old man remembers where he is, how he got here, how it is that the great Achilles, already dressed and armed, is here beside his bed.

'There is warm water,' Achilles tells him.

Two servants, one with a pitcher, the other bearing a bowl and cloth, are standing a little way off, in the half-light under the portico awning. The younger of them yawns and looks quickly to see if Achilles has seen it. The other makes a clicking sound of half-indulgent disapproval.

For some reason this exchange between the two, which has caught Priam's new-found eye for such irrelevant happenings, has an enlivening effect, brings him back into the world with a renewed sense of how full it is of the odd and engaging, and of things to be dealt with and done. He pushes back the covers and, wincing a little as he swings his legs over the side of the cot, gets slowly to his feet, then stands with his eyes closed, waiting for the pain in his hip joint to ease.

Achilles is impressed again by the man's long bones, and the remains in him of a commanding strength, as, very elegantly but without fuss, he holds his cupped hands over the basin while Alcimus pours, then vigorously splashes water over his head, all the while making little huffing sounds of pleasurable effort. Then accepts the cloth that is offered him, and stands quietly musing, the cloth in his hand, his brow dripping.

What has struck Priam is the strangeness of the moment.

The wolf's hour, deep in the Achaean camp.

In the distance, a clacking sound: the masts of the Greek ships, away there in the fog, tapping and creaking where they are drawn up in squadrons along the shore.

These attendant strangers with pitcher, bowl and cloth.

And the killer of his son, dread Achilles, standing wrapped in his cloak and watching, as with the sleep barely out of his eyes he dries his fingers, and the rapidly cooling water he has poured over his head drips and darkens the boards of the portico.

All this has the quality of a dream, where in just this way events and objects seem at once both puzzling and glowingly familiar.

But this is no dream. The cramp in his old bones tells him that, and the bulking presence that watches from just feet away: the animal eyes in the broad-browed skull; the big knuckles of the hand, which even in rest, lightly clasped now on the haft of his sword, retains a terrible potential.

What puzzles him is the desire he feels – curiosity again, that new impulse in him – to know more of what is hidden and contrary in this boldest, most ferocious, most unpredictable of the Greeks. Mightn't that be useful to him later? As a means to saving them – Hecuba, himself, his people – from what otherwise must surely come?

It is in the light of this *otherwise* that he stands with his brow dripping, while Achilles, who is also puzzled, looks on.

At their late night supper he had been treated with the utmost courtesy. Achilles himself had gone out to choose a good-sized hog, and when it had been brought in and laid on a board, had himself, in honour of his royal guest, jointed the chine and laid the pieces, sprinkled with salt, on the fire-dogs to be roasted.

At the small table in the empty hut – for the Myrmidons had been quietly dismissed – with Automedon and Alcimus to bring in the dishes and mix the wine, they had soon settled on the terms of a truce.

Nine days for the Trojans to make a journey into the forests of Mount Ida and fell the pine logs for Hector's pyre. In the city, nine days of ceremonial mourning. On the tenth the burning of Hector's body. The eleventh for the raising of his burial mound. On the twelfth the war would resume.

But it was the eleven days of peace that Priam had felt shining around them as they dipped their hands into the bowl and quietly talked.

Days of sorrow, but also of holiday from the din and dread of battle. A time for living.

Quietly, as they ate together, he and Achilles had discovered a kind of intimacy; wary at first, though also respectful, and at last quite easy, though Priam had continually to remind himself who it was he was breaking bread with, and what lay out there wrapped in a sheet and waiting to be reclaimed.

He had eaten little, but for form's sake had taken something from each dish.

Achilles, urged on by Automedon, ate heartily, the fingers of his huge hands running with the juices of the meat, and for a moment, as the tight jaw worked, Priam had seen quite clearly the whole terrible machinery of the man, though all their talk was of peace.

So now, refreshed by sleep and by the water he has splashed over his head, Priam turns and they go down together to the yard.

The wagon is already loaded and waiting, the driver beside it, the two mules quiet in the shafts. The little one, Priam is pleased to see, knows him now, and when he scratches her on the top of the head, rubs her ear against his sleeve. In the bed of the wagon, under a rich mantle, the body of his son.

He walks past it, allowing the practice of long years, a lifetime of rigorous discipline, to hide from these invaders what he feels. He extends his hand to his good Idaeus to be helped up.

Surprised again by how quickly all this has grown pleasant and familiar to him. The driver's calloused hand clutching his own, the two mules, now that they are ready to set off, beginning to be restive and dancing about on the frosty ground. Even the discomfort of the wooden crossbench, which is so hard on an old man's bones, is a homecoming.

Achilles and his two squires, walking in a group beside the cart, accompany them to the open gate. Groups of guards, newly risen, move about among their cook-fires, looking puzzled as the cart, with its escort, rumbles by them and comes to a halt before the gate. Achilles, at Priam's side, rests his hand a moment on the support of the canopy.

'Call on me, Priam,' he says lightly, 'when the walls of Troy are falling around you, and I will come to your aid.'

It is their moment of parting.

Priam pauses, and the cruelty of the answer that comes to his lips surprises him.

'And if, when I call, you are already among the shades?'

Achilles feels a chill pass through him. It is cold out here.

'Then alas for you, Priam, I will not come.'

It is, Achilles knows, a joke of the kind the gods delight in, who joke darkly. Smiling in the fore-knowledge of what they have already seen, both of them, he lifts his hand, and on a word from the driver the cart jolts on out of the camp.

The sun is already up and has begun to burn off the crisp white groundfrost as they leave the stockade wall behind them. Little birds are twittering in the fog, which crawls so close to the ground that they seem to be setting out across a lake which stretches shoreless in all directions. The carter leans forward over the traces. Calling softly to his mules, he pulls them this way and that as their feet seek out the road.

On either side as they pass, the barrows of the dead. Ghostly figures materialise for a moment among them, then dissolve. Old men and small children are out gathering kindling, which they pile in armfuls onto handcarts or lash to their backs in tottering bundles. The women are scavenging for battle relics – a silver pin, the clasp off a pair of greaves. All this part of the plain has been the scene, at one time or another, of skirmishes or pitched battles in which hundreds of men have fallen and been dragged away.

The women move close to the earth, their hands turning the clods, breaking them up with practised fingers. Too absorbed in their task to care for the cart that looms up out of the fog and rumbles past them.

Later, with the fog-trails thinning and weak sunlight warm on their back, they pass the remains of a village – the charred stumps of an olive grove and a dozen smoke-blackened roofless huts. Half a dozen ragged infants, big-eyed and pot-bellied, come out to stare at them. One, a little girl of three or four, holds out her hand as if begging, but makes no effort to approach.

They go on in silence, slowly, till the sun is high above the horizon and they are clear at last of the camp and all its outposts. Then:

'Here,' Priam says quietly. 'Stop here.'

They are nowhere, as far as the carter can see – in a desolate dry stretch of brush and waist-high mallow – but he pulls at the traces, calls to his mules, and they come to a halt.

Priam, refusing help, climbs down, walks round to the bed of the cart and at last lifts the coverlet from the face of his son.

The carter continues to sit. Joggling the traces lightly in his hand, he gazes fixedly ahead.

Off in the distance, the hills towards Troy are just beginning to develop shadows on their sides; their crests are already touched with gold. Behind him he hears the small sounds Priam is making. They are wordless but he understands them well enough. His thoughts go to the long night he spent, he and the boy's mother, when they brought his eldest son home and they had sat together in the uncertain lamplight on either side of the broken body. Wordless but not silent.

He snuffles, rubs his nose with the back of his wrist and pulls a little at the left-hand trace, so that Beauty turns her head, just enough for him to catch sight of her round eye, its clear glistening white.

Their adventure is nearly over. In no time now, he tells himself, I will be back in my own life. And he thinks, with a burst of joy, of the little girl, his grand-daughter, now fully recovered; how she will come running on her fat little legs to meet him when he rounds the big rock at the bottom of their hill and begins the slow climb to the village. Somewhere along the way he must find something to bring her. Then tomorrow he will go as usual with his cart and his two mules and wait to be hired in the marketplace.

Behind him, Priam falls silent. After a little he comes round to the step of the wagon and without speaking reaches his hand up to be helped.

They go on. Nothing is said. The sun grows warmer. The hot damp smell of earth comes to their nostrils.

After his moment of turmoil Priam has settled. The air is fresh and clear. The cart rolls along at a good pace now, lighter than on the journey out. This is triumph.

It is only a provisional triumph, of course; the gods are not to be trusted when they tilt the balance momentarily in your favour. And what sort of triumph is it to be bringing home the body of a son? But he has done something for which he will be remembered for as long as such stories are told. He has stepped into a space that till now was uninhabited and found a way to fill it. Not as he filled his old role as king, since all he had to do in that case was follow convention, slip his arms into the sleeves of an empty garment and stand still, but as one for whom every gesture had still to be hit upon, every word discovered anew, to say nothing of the conviction needed to carry all to its conclusion. He has done that and is coming home, even in these last days of his life, as a man remade.

Look, he wants to shout, I am still here, but the *I* is different. I come as a man of sorrow bringing the body of my son for burial, but I come also as a hero of the deed that till now was never attempted.

He does not think of this as a beginning; or not, anyway, of something large. How could it be? What lies ahead is the interim of the truce, a time for ordinary life to be resumed, one day then the next; no more than that can be counted on. But in his present mood it is enough.

They arrive again at the slope that leads down, through sycamore figs and holm oak, to the fording place with its two channels, one milky, the other leaping clear over sunlit stones; between them the sandbanks with their clumps of flowering bay.

They lurch into the stream, and the driver gets

down to urge his mules through the waist-high current, then onto the gravel and humped sand of the island midstream. Back in the cart, he takes them more easily through the second current, which is fast-running but comes barely to their hocks. Then up the gently sloping bank.

The screen of tamarisks stirs and shimmers but they do not stop there, and no god is lounging in the shade. They are coming home. No need this time for a guide or safe-conduct.

But Priam thinks with affection now of that earlier occasion. Of the water, and how it cooled his feet when he sat with his robe bunched in his lap and let them soak. And of the fishlings. And how good the little griddlecakes had tasted, and of the young woman who made them – well-favoured, he had a god's word for that, even if she did go limping. All this as warm in his memory as some moment recalled from childhood, with a whole life lived between, though in fact it happened just hours ago.

They are almost home now. As they emerge from the treeline that marks the course of the river, Troy, with its walls and battlements – far off, but not so far – is visible on its bluff. Tiny specks, which are swallows, weave in close circles round its towers and in larger circles in the air above it, soaring to the pure blue heavens.

Riding towards it, the earth swarming and singing to the horizon, the wheels of the cart rumbling and the feet of the mules making a regular clopping sound on the road, which has by now become a highway, Priam thinks how those walls, in the days of King Laomedon, his father, had been raised to music struck from the hands of a god, and feels his homecoming now as the coming home to a state of exultant wellbeing in which he too is divinely led as by music.

In his hut Achilles too is visited by a lightness that is both new and a return. Bodily action, the dance of the blood in the play of hand, foot, eye, seems once again the exercise of spirit in him. His heels glow. His sword, when he lifts it, is metal from the depths of the earth made solid flame. In the instant warmth and energy that fills him, the end, which is so close now, seems to have been miraculously suspended.

It has not.

The boy Neoptolemus is no longer in his grand-father's house in Scyros being spoiled by women. The bronze-haired avenger of his father's death, already filled with the fierce light of the future, is at sea and sailing fast for Troy.

A child of time, he knows already that the last days of this story belong to him. He cannot wait to burst through the doors and come hurtling into the honeycomb, the maze, the hundred rooms of Priam's palace, to where the old man standing dazed beside the altar at its centre turns an assent-ing gaze upon him. The rest is headlong and bloody but unfolds with the effortlessness of trance – that is how the youthful hero sees it, and how he has lived it through long days of training in boyish dreams. But the moment, when it arrives, is not at all like that.

Priam has tripped in flight on the hem of his robe and lies sprawled on the palace floor. He casts a terrified glance behind him as the furious boy descends, flame-headed, enraged, his body a fur-nace pouring out heat, a round mouth shouting. What the mouth proclaims is instant night.

The youth himself can barely stand, he is already so drunk with slaughter, and a panicky fear assails him that in the excitement of the moment he may fall out of his wrathful dream. 'Father,' his soul whispers towards a figure he barely recalls. To be son to the great Achilles is a burden.

All scrag and bones, the old man he has fallen upon, like a dog that has to be put down and refuses to go quietly, half-rises and wrestles in his grip. He wrenches sideways, resisting the blade, and the boy, for all his ready strength and sinew, and the hardness and agility of youth, grunts with the effort and grows breathless. His heart is racing. His palms are slippery with sweat.

Awkwardly aspraddle, he cries out like a child in his frustration – this is ridiculous! – and tugs the head back hard in his locked forearm, his right hand hacking at cartilage. He repeats the cry and hacks and hacks. Warm blood jerks over his fist.

'Father,' he whispers again, and to his horror – he feels the short hairs bristle on the back of his neck – the old bundle he is grappling to his chest, out of some other occasion, or some other life or history, turns upon him a ghastly far-off smile; then, with a last spasm and a hollow, hideous rattling of his breath, subsides, and the air is filled with the stench of shit.

Still panting, the boy sits up. Thrusts the old man from him. Glances fearfully about. At least there is no one here to see it. To see the botch he has made of things. Still in a daze, his gorged heart pounding, he pushes slowly to his feet.

The paving all around and under him is slick with blood. He hangs upright, shoulders drooping, hands thick and heavy at the ends of his wrists. The rush of exhilaration that had claimed him has leaked away. In a sudden swift reversal is replaced by crushing disappointment; heartsickness, animal sadness, despondency. Nothing here has gone cleanly or as he wished. All botched! All scramble and boyish hot confusion. His chin sunk on his breast, 'Pardon me, father,' he whispers. Hot tears sully his cheeks.

And for him the misery of this moment will last forever; that is the hard fact he must live with. However the story is told and elaborated, the raw shame of it will be with him now till his last breath.

But time has not yet reached that point. The blood still warm and ticking in his wrist, Priam raises an arm and points towards the walls of his city and to a figure standing small and emphatic against the light.

'There,' he tells the driver. 'Do you see her?'

The carter nods, but is lost in his own concerns.

He must find something in the market for his little one. A pair of earrings perhaps, or a child's painted cart like his own – she would like that – to wheel up and down the floor of their hut. Something too for the daughter-in-law – more difficult, this – to celebrate his homecoming, and to mark this day and night he has just passed that has been so extraordinary and which he owes to Beauty. He will find something for Beauty as well, and for Shock, who cannot help, poor creature, that he is unremarkable and has no special charm.

Pricked with conscience by the ingratitude of this, he leans forward and scratches Shock's ear with the traces; then, so that Beauty will not be jealous, tickles her ear as well.

As for all that has happened in these last hours, what a tale he will have to tell! He will tell it often over the years.

In the early days, while Troy still stands solid and gleaming on its high hill, the figures he has to speak of, Priam, Hecuba, Achilles, will still, in the minds of his listeners, be sharers of their own world, creatures like themselves of flesh and blood. Later – when Troy has become just another long, windswept hilltop, its towers reduced to rubble, its citizens scattered or carried off, like Hecuba and Hector's wife Andromache and Cassandra and the other Trojan women, into exile and slavery – all he has to tell, which was once as real as the itch under his tunic and the lice he cracks between his nails, will have become the stuff of legend, half folktale, half an old man's empty bragging.

Even the memory then, of what once was, will have grown dim in the minds of a generation who, for the whole of their lives, have known nothing but chaos and lawlessness. Roads impassable and, where they are not, controlled by petty warlords who demand toll-fees at every ford, or freebooters intent on robbery or worse. No village, however securely walled, safe now from the bands of long-haired brigands and marauders who, as soon as the snows have begun to melt, erupt out of mountain passes to rob farmers of the last of their grain, to fire barns, steal women and cattle, and kidnap children as new recruits to their footloose empire of flame and pillage.

So many stories!

He tells them to anyone who will share a drink with him. On summer evenings under the big misshapen sycamore at the tavern door, nodding off at times in mid-sentence so that his listeners creep away smiling and shake their heads. Or by the light of a single oil lamp, and with a young one on his lap – one of his many great-grandchildren – on long nights when the entire village is holed up against invaders behind the doors of a fortified barn.

Those who sit, intent as children, and give themselves up to these old tales, will have heard them a hundred times before and know every detail and unlikely turn.

The meeting in the tamarisk grove with the impudent fellow who was, in fact, the god Hermes in the guise of an Achaean warrior: a dandified youth with golden tresses, and a scent – it was this that had given him away – like gillyflowers.

How, in a quiet spot beyond the same tamarisk grove, he had managed, without too much trouble, to tempt the old king, Priam, who had never heard of such a thing, to cool his feet in the running stream, and taste one of the little griddlecakes his daughter-in-law was such a dab hand at.

How he had spent the night in the open yard beside Achilles' hut in the Greek camp, and was given gobbets of meat to eat that the great Achilles himself had sliced and roasted. With scallions, and the finest wheaten bread to soak up the grease. And had slept very comfortably afterwards under a lambswool rug provided by one of Achilles' squires.

His listeners do not believe him, of course. He is a known liar. He is a hundred years old and drinks too much.

What he has to tell did happen – or so they say – but to someone else. Idaeus, the man was called, King Priam's herald. Is it likely that such a figure, a king's herald, would have griddlecakes in his satchel? Do great kings dabble their feet in icy streams?

This old fellow, like most storytellers, is a stealer of other men's tales, of other men's lives. The whole of his own life he has spent as a poor day labourer. He is, as everyone knows, a carter who, long ago, when there was a town hereabouts, went out each morning to offer himself for hire in the marketplace, carrying household goods from one ward to another, and hay or stone or firewood to nearby villages. The most remarkable thing about him was that he was the owner of a little black mule who is still remembered in this part of the country and much talked about. A charming creature, big-eyed and sleek, she bore the name of Beauty – and very appropriately too, it seems, which is not always the case.

AFTERWORD

A note on sources

One rainy Friday afternoon in 1943, when we were unable to go out into the playground for our usual period of tunnel ball, our primary-school teacher, Miss Finlay, read us a story. It was the Troy story. For some reason, though I was a keen reader, I had never heard it, and when the bell rang and Miss Finlay dismissed us with the story left hanging, I was devastated.

We too were in the middle of a war. Brisbane, where I lived, was the headquarters of General MacArthur's Pacific campaign and the jumping-off place for hundreds of thousands of American and other troops on their way to the north. The city buildings were sandbagged, their windows crisscrossed with sticky-tape against the possibility of their shattering during a raid. I had immediately connected Miss Finlay's ancient and fictional war with our own. We too were left hanging in the midst of an unfinished war. Who could know, in 1943, how our war too might end?

Thirty years later, in a poem called 'Episode from an Early War', still haunted by the characters in Miss Finlay's story, I tried to bring the two parts of my experience together:

Sometimes, looking back, I find myself, a bookish
          nine-
year-old, still gazing down
through the wartime criss-cross shock-
proof glass of my suburban primary school.
          Blueflint gravel
ripples in my head, the schoolyard throbs. And
          all the players
of rip-shirt rough-and-tumble
wargames stop, look on in stunned surprise:
Hector, hero of Troy,
raw-bloody-boned is dragged across the scene
and pissed on and defiled,
while myrmidons of black flies crust his wounds
          and the angelic
blunt-faced ones, the lords of mutilation,
haul off and watch.

Thirty years later again, *Ransom* is a return to that unfinished story; to my discovery, once in 1943, once again in 1972, that

> . . . the war, our war,
> was real: highways of ash
> where ghostly millions rise out of their shoes and
>   go barefoot
> nowhere . . .

It re-enters the world of the *Iliad* to recount the story of Achilles, Patroclus and Hector, and, in a very different version from the original, Priam's journey to the Greek camp. But its primary interest is in storytelling itself – why stories are told and why we need to hear them, how stories get changed in the telling – and much of what it has to tell are 'untold tales' found only in the margins of earlier writers.

The story of how Patroclus came to be the friend and companion of Achilles occupies only half a dozen lines in the *Iliad*; the bare facts of how a small survivor of war, Podarces, came to be Priam ('the ransomed one' or 'the price paid'), King of Troy, an equally brief passage, referring to the exploits of Hercules, in *The Library*, a history of mythology sometimes attributed, falsely it seems, to Apollodorus (born *c.* 180 BC). How a simple carter, Somax, for one day became the Trojan herald Idaeus, and Priam's companion on his journey to the Greek camp, appears for the first time in the pages of this book.

My thanks to Alison Samuel at Chatto & Windus in London, to Meredith Curnow and Julian Welch at Knopf, Sydney, and yet again to Chris Edwards, whose encouragement, and keen eye and ear, have been essential to *Ransom* from its earliest completed draft.

ABOUT THE AUTHOR

David Malouf is the author of, among other works, *Dream Stuff, Remembering Babylon, An Imaginary Life,* and *The Conversations at Curlow Creek*. Honors he has received include the IMPAC Dublin Literary Award, the Australia-Asia Literary Award, the Prix Femina Étranger, and the Los Angeles Times Book Award. He lives in Australia.